BEAUTY
AND THE BOSS

BEAUTY
AND THE BOSS

USA TODAY BESTSELLING AUTHOR
DIANE ALBERTS

Entangled Publishing
644 Shrewsbury Commons Ave
STE 181
Shrewsbury, PA 17361
rights@entangledpublishing.com

Indulgence is an imprint of Entangled Publishing.

Edited by Candace Havens
Cover design by LJ Anderson/Mayhem Cover Creations
Cover photography by South_agency/iStock

Manufactured in the United States of America

First Edition November 2015

This one goes out to all those readers out there who love the story of Beauty and the Beast as much as I do.

Chapter One

Benjamin Gale III rubbed his temples, let out an exasperated sigh, and then leaned back in his chair. The sun had already faded to a dull orange glow, and the sky darkened over the famous New York City skyline with each passing moment, but he was still working his ass off, and probably would be for another few hours, at the very least. He didn't really have a choice.

His family was trying to wrestle control of the company, and he'd be damned if he was going to allow that to happen without a hell of a fight. This was his life. His wife. His world. His baby. He'd dedicated the last five years to this office.

And it belonged to *him*.

If they wanted to take control of Gale Incorporated out of his hands, they'd have to pry it out with the use of deadly force. If there was one thing he got from his mother—who despised him—it was her stubborn determination to win.

And he would damn well win.

Hell, he knew why his mother hated him, and even understood it. He'd fucked up years ago, when his father died, and she blamed him for it. If it made her happy to hate him, if it made missing her husband a little easier on her, then more power to her. But now she wanted to take *his* company away from him? His own birthright?

Not in this damn lifetime. Or the next.

Over the five years since his father had passed away, he'd dedicated his life to trying to make things right. He'd quit partying. Stopped fucking around, and his whole life had been focused on this. On his *work*. And if he wasn't *at* work, he was attending a function *for* work. He spent every moment of every waking hour being the man his father would have wanted him to be. He'd been dedicated, studious, and predictable as hell.

All his friends had abandoned him. Called him boring.

It was true. He *was*.

He even lived in the penthouse upstairs to be close to his office at all hours. His entire life existed in this damn Beacon Court building. If that wasn't dedication, he wasn't sure what was. But still—it wasn't enough. It would never be—

"What are you doing?" one of his employees asked. He straightened out of reflex, but she was outside the door, not in his office. "Why are you still here?"

"I'm not finished with my report yet," he heard Maggie Donovan, his lead researcher, say. She had the most angelic voice he'd ever known, and she was perpetually kind and always smiling. Pretty much the opposite of him. "You heading out?"

"Yeah. Everyone is."

"Well, I'm not," Maggie said, clearing her throat. "I'll be here for a little while longer, so go ahead without me."

"Why do you always stay late?" the other employee asked—and for the life of him, he couldn't remember her name. She worked on the left side of the office, and had brown hair, but that's all he remembered. "The beast doesn't appreciate it, or you."

He stiffened. The beast, of course, was him.

All of his employees called him that. They thought he wasn't aware of it, but he kept up to date on everything that happened outside of his executive office.

"Don't call him that," Maggie hissed, her voice dropping lower. "He's not a beast, he's just a guy who—"

Her voice was too low for him to hear the rest, but that was just as well. He didn't need to hear another damn word. His employees could hate him all they wanted, as long as they turned their fucking work in on time. But the fact that Maggie defended him? It made him like her even more than he already did.

Which was an anomaly, since he didn't really like *anyone*. Not anymore.

Picking up his phone, he pushed the button that rang directly into his apartment. His butler answered. "What can I do for you, sir?"

"Hey, Willie."

"Willie?" William, his elderly and very British butler, let out a long, annoyed sigh. "I don't know anyone who goes by that name, sir."

He laughed. This was a game they played, and Willie was a good sport about it. "Fine. *William*."

"What can I do for you, sir?"

"Can you send some dinner down for me now? Mr. Forbes should be here any minute." He checked the time. Quarter till seven. "What is it tonight?"

"Eggplant parmesan, sir." Disapproval was clear in his tone. "Working late *again*?"

"Yep. I'm the only one here besides—" He sat up straighter and cleared his throat, his mind still on Maggie Donovan and her defense of him, which was really quite admirable since he'd never given her a reason to think well of him. After all the times he'd made her stay late, which she did without a shred of complaining, the least he could do was have some dinner delivered to her desk as a thanks. "Actually, I'd like three orders sent down, please. And don't forget the wine. Red."

"Right away, sir."

He set the phone in the receiver and glanced at the door again. Out there, just a few steps away, was Maggie. While he'd never act on it, the attraction was there. There had always been something about her that made him think of her way too often, considering she was his employee—and a damn good one. She was gorgeous as hell, her smile lit up a room, and she had a body that could easily inspire a rock ballad.

But Maggie—she was different.

Yeah, she was gorgeous, but he was fairly certain she didn't have a clue. And when she smiled, sometimes she scrunched up her face, and those three little freckles across her nose danced. Her long, wavy brown hair and blue eyes—so dark they were more smoky gray than blue, really—haunted him when he was in bed alone.

Not that he'd noticed.

There was just something about her he couldn't explain. He'd give anything to have her turn one of those bright smiles on him—preferably while naked and screaming out his name—but she was his employee, and he was her boss, and such things weren't allowed in his office.

Yet another reason he was the Beast of Gale.

He had a strict policy against dating in the office. It was necessary if he wanted his employees to focus on their work and not each other.

But with Maggie, it might be worth—

Tugging on his tie again, he stood, walked over to his minibar, poured himself a shot of Macallan, and downed it. He needed to stop that train of thought before it even left the station. Fucking around with Maggie wasn't something his father would have ever done. It wouldn't get the investors his mother had in her pocket off his back, either. Ever since she'd received her cut of the company shares, she'd been a... nuisance, to say the least.

And at this point in the fight to retain control as CEO, he couldn't afford to fuck up over a pretty face and a sexy smile. After he poured another drink, he walked to the window, staring down at the dark city from ten stories up. Cars honked, sirens screeched, and steam rose from the subway. A couple fought at the corner of Fifty-eighth and Lexington, and across the street, another couple kissed.

The energy from watching all the lives that intertwined and intersected made him feel...*alive*. Even though he wasn't the one out there actually living, he loved it anyway. All those people down there were so free. So original. So impulsively thriving.

Everything *he* could never be.

His phone rang, tearing him from his thoughts, and he crossed the room to pick it up. "Gale."

"It's Carl. Carl Forbes."

Benjamin sank into his desk chair and rolled his eyes at the formal greeting. His father's old work crony was nothing if not old-fashioned. "Hey, I was just watching out the window, checking to see if I could spot that ugly old yellow Jag of yours coming down the road yet. You're late, old man."

Carl chuckled. "You wouldn't recognize beauty if it punched you in the face, son."

Oh, but he did. One of the most beautiful women he'd ever seen sat outside his office, working on a Friday night, probably cursing his name with every breath. He'd rather make her out of breath for better reasons. "I beg to differ, sir."

"Well, regardless, you won't be seeing it. I have to cancel.

My knee's giving me trouble, and it's supposed to be icy tonight. The old lady won't let me leave."

He sighed. There went his "exciting" Friday night plans. Not that they'd been much to write home about, since his plans had been eating in the office with a sixty-five-year-old man, and then returning to work. "I completely understand, Carl."

After they rescheduled and exchanged a few more words, Benjamin hung up. No sooner had he set the phone down than he heard voices outside his door again, this time Maggie and his butler. Sighing, he moved his empty glass to the bar.

The door opened, and William carried in a tray with three covered plates, an open carafe of wine he'd never finish on his own, and two glasses. "Good evening, sir."

"Wow, that was quick, Willie. Might be a new record." He checked his Rolex. "Five minutes?"

William cracked a smile at the nickname he "despised," and set the tray on the table by the window. "Last week we made it down here in under four and a half—but that was only with one meal."

"Impressive," he drawled, grinning as he rolled up his shirtsleeves. Willie was the only person he truly relaxed around. "Thanks, man."

"You're welcome, sir." Willie straightened and smoothed his gray, balding hair. "Shall I send for whomever this third dinner is for?"

"Oh. No. I've got it." He stopped mid-roll. "I'll tell her myself."

William bowed, but his eyes lit up at the mention of a female. "Very well, sir. I'll see you when you come up."

"Thanks," Benjamin said, smiling at the old man, who'd been there for him since the moment he'd taken his first breath. "Don't wait up. It'll be another late night."

"Very well, sir."

After the butler left, he straightened the table, picked up one of the plates, and made it halfway across the office before he froze. He had all this wine, and all this food. Why not invite her to eat *with* him? Sure, it might not be proper, from a boss-employee perspective, but no one would find out.

It wasn't as if he was going to fuck her over his desk, no matter how much he might wish he could. And it *was* Friday night. It seemed such a damn shame to waste the bread and wine. Despite what everyone said, he wasn't a beast, and he did like Maggie. He wasn't heartless. He was *motivated*.

Back before his father had died, Benjamin had lived hard, partied harder, and laughed loudly. Now, he tried to pretend that version of him never existed, and he did his damnedest to be the man he should have been back then. Sometimes it felt as if that younger Benjamin had died, leaving a stranger in his place.

A man that he didn't even like. A man *no one* liked.

Yet Maggie had still defended him. She had a pure heart. A kind nature. And he wanted to repay that kindness. It wasn't going to redeem him or make him a good man, but damn it, it was *some*thing. She deserved a hot, fresh meal. End of story.

Before he could talk himself out of it, he walked to his office door, took a deep breath, and opened it. Sure enough, she still sat there, working diligently.

Like usual.

Her small foot tapped against the front of her desk, and she hummed a tune under her breath. She wore a pair of square, black glasses, her hair was frazzled, and she nibbled on her pen with that red mouth of hers, which had starred in way too many of his fantasies. The dark sky behind her was lit up by buildings and streetlights.

But she was the thing that really shone.

His heart quickened ridiculously, and he took a deep

breath as his pants grew uncomfortably tight. She truly had a beauty that was incomparable and indescribable. He shifted his weight and cleared his throat, forcing his face to take on the stoic mask he wore around his employees—hell, around *everyone*. "Ms. Donovan?"

She glanced up, jumped, and dropped the pen on her desk. As she rose to her feet unsteadily, he fought back a smile. She always acted surprised when he actually acknowledged her, or dared to exit his office, as if she'd forgotten she wasn't alone, or that he even existed. It was endearing, and tonight wasn't any exception.

"Sir?" she asked. "I'm still working on—"

"I know." He glanced down at her disheveled desk. All her personal items were scattered about the top of it, and her pens weren't in any sort of color-coded order at all. It made his fingers itch to straighten it up for her, but he stood still. It wasn't his job to make her desk organized. "I was wondering if you were hungry?"

She darted a glance to the door, then back at him. "I packed dinner. I just haven't gotten around to heating it up yet."

"Oh. Well, my dinner plans were canceled last minute." He pointed over his shoulder. "If you'd rather, I have fresh eggplant parmesan and wine, and it's still hot—if that's agreeable to you."

"Agreeable?"

Again, the urge to smile hit him. He didn't. "Dinner. With me."

"Umm..." Blinking, she tucked her hair behind her ear, took it out, and tucked it in again. He'd obviously made her nervous. "Let me get this straight. You're inviting me to dinner? With you? Alone?"

He raised a brow. "I just said that, didn't I?"

"Uh." She stepped around her desk, clasping her hands

in front of her nervously. "Yeah, I guess so. Are you sure? I mean, you're the boss and—"

"You're a great employee. I thought you might like to eat dinner." He tugged on his tie. "That's all, Maggie."

She choked on a laugh at his use of her first name. Whenever she got nervous, she laughed. Yet another thing he found adorable about her. "I mean, yeah, I like food."

His lips quirked. "Good."

"Yeah." She smiled at him. "Uh, good."

He crossed his arms and watched her through his lowered lids. Her white button-up shirt strained over her generous breasts, and her black pencil skirt hugged the curve of her hips. It was prim and proper office attire, and yet she somehow managed to make it look drop-dead-sexy without even trying. It was fucking ridiculous. "If it makes you uncomfortable, please don't hesitate to say no. I won't be insulted."

"It doesn't make me uncomfortable at all," she said softly, her head tilted. He loved how she stared him straight in the eye and didn't cower away from him like the rest of the staff, and how the smile never faded from her lips. "I just didn't want to create the wrong impression, is all. I mean, we're alone, and if we're eating, if might look like a...well, you know."

"A date?"

"Yes. That." She pointed at him as if he'd given her the correct answer in a game show. He half expected her to announce that he'd moved on to the next round. "People might get the wrong idea."

He lifted a hand and encompassed the empty office. "Yes, clearly gossip would be an issue."

"Okay." She glanced around, and one side of her mouth quirked up higher than the other. "You got me there. Eggplant parm, huh?"

"Yep." He stepped back and gestured her inside his office. "And wine, too, if you're feeling adventurous."

"I'm not done with the report yet," she said quickly, her cheeks flushing to a fetching pink as she headed toward him, smoothing her skirt. "I'll have to return to work after I eat."

"Leave it."

She blinked. "But—"

"I said, leave it." He left the door open, just in case someone happened to come in after hours. When she stood at the table awkwardly, he pulled a chair out, and watched her. She sat down, and he pushed her in closer to the table. She let out a little gasp and clutched the edge of her seat. "It'll wait till Monday," he said.

"Maybe I can take it home with me and work on it over the weekend," she said, placing a white linen napkin on her lap with a perfectly manicured hand. "It's not my style to just leave things undone."

"Mine either." He sat down and lifted the cover from her dinner plate. After setting it down, he picked up the bottle of Clos Du Val pinot noir, and leaned in. Her nose was inches from his, and she watched him with wide eyes. He had the undeniable urge to lean in even more and capture her mouth with his. Of course, he didn't, but still. The impulse was there. "So let's be rebellious together, Maggie."

She let out a nervous laugh, tucking her hair behind her ear. "Okay. Sure. Why not? Pour the wine, sir."

"I like a woman who can see the merits of letting loose every once in a while," he said.

She blinked at him, lowered her head, and straightened her napkin. "I don't let loose very often."

"I doubt that's true." He lifted a brow. "Surely when you're at home, with your boyfriend, you—"

She lifted a hand, cutting him off. "I'll stop you right there. There's no boyfriend at home. As lame as it might sound, there's just a cat."

Satisfaction over her answer punched him in the chest, but he'd ignore that and the reason for it, too, thank you very fucking much. "I don't even have that."

"The boyfriend?" She smiled, looking more at ease. "Or the cat?"

"Either one." He picked up the wine. "Tell me, how long ago did you move to New York?"

She scrunched her nose, making those freckles dance. "Is it that obvious I'm not a native?"

"Yeah." He poured her a glass. "Sorry."

She laughed and blew out a breath. Her bangs fluttered, but fell right back into her sight. "No apologies needed. I'm sure I stick out like a sore thumb."

"You're very polite and you apologize too much." He poured himself a glass, too, and held it up. "But that's not necessarily a bad thing."

She clinked her glass to his, and took a sip. He lifted his glass just as she muttered, "He says with an apologetic tone…"

Choking on his wine, he set the glass down and swallowed hard. "Did you seriously just *narrate* our conversation?"

"Um, maybe?" She flushed. "I talk to myself a lot. It's a bad habit."

Or a delightful one.

Setting his glass down, he picked up his fork, unable to tear his eyes off of her. Her knee brushed his under the table and she jerked it back right away, shooting a quick glance at him. He didn't miss the flush in her cheeks, or her quickened breath at the contact, but damn it, he wished he had. *Still not fucking touching her, Gale.* "You do?"

"I just said so, didn't I?"

Fighting back a grin at her saucy tone, he shook his head. She'd turned his earlier words around on him. He'd always been a sucker for a quick wit, and the fact that she didn't treat him like he was her boss, or the Beast of Gale, sat well with him. The rest of the workers tiptoed around him as if he might bite their heads off.

They weren't exactly wrong.

He probably wasn't the easiest boss in the world, but he didn't demand anything from anyone that he didn't ask from himself. "I don't willingly say this about a lot of people, but I like you, Maggie."

She flushed even more. "Uh—why?"

"For starters, you're not afraid of me." He swallowed a bite of eggplant parmesan. It was perfection. Chef Antoine had outdone himself. "It's refreshing."

She raised her brows and cut into her own dinner. "What's to be afraid of?"

"I guess it's because I'm a beast."

She choked on her food, swallowed it, and reached for her wine with a shaking hand. He watched her with amusement as she drank the whole glass. Once finished, she set it down and locked eyes with him. "So, you heard that?"

He nodded once. "I also heard you defend me. Thank you."

"Oh. That?" She waved a hand. "That was nothing. It's ridiculous that they gave you that name in the first place. You being a strict boss doesn't make you scary."

"If you say so."

"I do." She licked her lips, and he couldn't look away from her red, exquisite mouth. Leaning in, she rested a small hand on his arm. Her innocent touch burned through his shirt, searing his skin, and he stiffened. Her nostrils flared slightly, and she held his arm tighter, as if she felt the instant attraction, too. His pulse sped up, and he shifted in his chair to accommodate his increasing hardness. "And anyone who thinks otherwise is a fool."

He wasn't sure how to answer that, so he didn't. "So, uh, where are you from originally?"

It had been years since he'd been this curious about a woman. She worked so hard. Never complained, and she was beautiful in a quiet and serene kind of way. She was nothing like the women he used to date—not that this was a date, nor was he even thinking about her that way. Okay, well, maybe a *bit*.

But they were just two people getting to know each other on a Friday night. At the office. He was rewarding her for her efforts. Yes, that's what this was.

That's *all* this was.

"A farm in South Dakota." She put her fork down and held a hand up. "You're shocked people actually live there, right?"

He swallowed a laugh. "Well, now that you mention it…"

"Oh, shut up," she said, laughing and tossing a piece of bread at him.

It hit his chest, exploding with crumbs before it fell into his lap. He blinked down at it. No one, in all his thirty-three years, had *ever* thrown food at him. He'd seen it in movies but didn't think people actually did it.

Something of his shock must have shown on his face, because she turned whiter than the table linen.

"Oh…" She jerked back, knocking her fork under the table. "Oh crap. I'm sorry, sir. So sorry. I forgot—"

He held up a hand. "It's fine. Your fork might not agree, but I'm good."

She laughed uneasily. "I'm such a klutz, give me a second." Scooting out the chair, she crawled under the table. Benjamin lost sight of her, but her hand brushed his ankle, which didn't do a lot of good for his dwindling resistance to her. "Oops."

He swept the breadcrumbs off his crisp dress shirt,

forcing his body to cool the hell off, and peeked at her under the table. She knelt at his feet, on all fours, and stared up at him. She rested a hand on his knee, laughing uneasily. "This isn't awkward *at all*, right? I mean, I'm just a girl, kneeling under a table at her boss's feet…"

An almost-laugh escaped him. "*Maggie*."

The moment they locked eyes, the air between them became charged, and the desire was undeniably there. Her hand on his knee tightened, and then she let go with a small sound. The way she looked at him—all wide eyes and parted lips—practically begged him to stop fighting the attraction between them.

To take what she had to offer, and more.

He cleared his throat. "You—"

"I—" she started.

"Am I interrupting?" A chilly voice he recognized all too well intercepted.

Well, *shit*.

"Not at all." He stiffened, fisting the dainty white napkin in his lap. He knew, just *knew*, his mother would immediately assume the worst as to why a woman was on her knees, under the table, in his office. "What are you doing here?"

"William informed me you were working late, so I decided to stop in. I see that working does not mean the same thing to me as it does you. No big surprise, of course."

He stood to give her a stiff half-bow of greeting. She was about to skin him alive, and he had only himself to blame. He never should have invited Maggie to dinner. "What a pleasant surprise, Mother."

"*Moth*—" Maggie straightened at his words, banging her head on the table. "*Ow*."

"Oh, Benjamin." She raised one haughty brown brow, curled her upper lip at his dinner companion, and hugged her Prada jacket closed. "I'll just bet it is."

Chapter Two

Maggie crawled out from under the table clutching her stupid fork, her face on fire and her heart racing. Out of all the positions to be found in, kneeling at her boss's feet was *not* the most flattering. And the thing was, she was the person least likely to be caught messing around with her *boss*. She had bad enough luck with men as it was; she wasn't about to throw the possibility of her ex firing her into the mix.

No, thank you.

She'd keep her disastrous romantic entanglements out of the office.

Once she made it to her feet with Mr. Gale's help—which his mother did *not* miss—she smoothed her skirt and swallowed hard, still clinging to the fork for dear life as if it could somehow save her from what was coming. "Mrs. Gale. This isn't—"

"Quiet," the older woman snapped, without taking her murderous glare off of her son. "No one was speaking to you."

Picking up her wine, she swallowed a healthy mouthful,

and it washed down the retort attempting to choke her to death in front of her boss and his nasty mother. The woman watched her son like he was a bug she'd stepped on.

Something to be scraped off and forgotten.

And, in return, Mr. Gale watched his mother with all the warmth of a winter's night. Maggie had never wanted the power to be invisible as much as she did right now.

And she used to pray for it every night.

Guess she knew now where he'd gotten his cold, emotionless exterior. He wasn't rude to her or anything. He *never* was. He just didn't really have the time, or the desire, to chat idly all day long. Something told her that he'd never been taught how.

They must not teach small talk at Harvard.

But they spent a lot of time alone at the office, so she got to see a side of him no one else did. And the more time she spent with him, the more he reminded her of a lost puppy who had all the bones in the world, but no idea what to do with them.

Especially after tonight.

"Please tell me this 'dinner' is not being billed to the company," Mrs. Gale said, each word icier than the last. "Last I checked, there is no clause in your contract that states the company must pay for your many dalliances."

Many dalliances?

She'd never have pegged Mr. Gale as a playboy.

Sure, he had the looks and the money to pull it off, but he spent almost all his time locked in his office, scowling out at his employees through the glass windows on either side of his closed door. *Alone.*

Covertly, she stole another glance at him as he shrugged back into his jacket while his mother watched him angrily. Tonight, he wore a black suit with a light green pinstripe dress shirt and a pair of black loafers. Something about the way his custom-made suit hugged all those hard muscles was a lot harder to ignore than it usually was—maybe because moments before she had been kneeling at his feet, staring up into his eyes and thinking how handsome he was from down there.

And he was. Handsome. From *every* angle.

Not just his feet.

He always had a slight five o'clock shadow going on, but she'd never seen his hair when it wasn't picture perfect. The man easily could have been a *GQ* model, but instead he was the CEO of his family's pharmaceutical company. He was well over six feet tall, weighed a little under two hundred pounds, was thirty-three years old, had attended Harvard for six years, and wore a size thirteen shoe.

I know way too much about him. Stalker.

She sighed.

Oh, and he was freakishly, devilishly, impossibly *hot*.

And single.

A muscle in his jaw ticked, but he remained otherwise motionless. "This isn't a 'dalliance', Mother," he said.

"It's not." Maggie tore her eyes off of him, flushing when his mother shot her a condescending look. "It's *so* not."

He shot her a narrow-eyed look.

She stared right back at him, and took a big gulp of wine.

The second he turned away, she put down her glass, swiped a napkin across her mouth, gently set her fork down, and decided to creep out while no one paid attention to her. If she had any luck—which she normally *didn't*—she'd escape before whatever was about to happen here happened. World War Three, maybe.

Slowly, she stepped sideways to the left.

Mrs. Gale snapped her fingers. "Sit down. No one excused you."

Before the sentence was even finished, Maggie slammed

her butt into the soft leather chair. Mr. Gale was her boss, which made his mother her even bigger boss, so she didn't exactly have a choice. "This really isn't what it looks like, Mrs. Gale. I—"

"Don't bother, Maggie." He frowned. "She won't believe you."

Mrs. Gale shrugged. "You're right. I won't."

He rubbed his jaw. "You can't come in here and order my employees around. If Maggie wants to leave, she's allowed. She's not a prisoner in my office."

She stood again. "Great. Thank you. I'll be on my—"

"Your employee?" The other woman laughed, but it didn't sound like humor at all. "Oh, that's just rich. You have one of your workers under your table doing...doing..."

Shoot me. Shoot me now.

"As we already told you," he said, his tone tight with exasperation. "It's not what it looked like."

"Oh, but it was. And there are rules against such things." Mrs. Gale focused her cold gaze on Maggie. "Get out. You're fired."

She exhaled a big breath of air, dread punching her in the stomach. She'd been in the city for half a year, fighting her way into this hard-to-attain position at Gale Incorporated, and now she'd been sacked over suspicion of going down on her hot boss—and she hadn't even done it. *Great. Just great.*

She had to get out of here, with her head held high, and then she'd cry. But not in front of this horrible woman. She nodded. "Right."

"Don't even think about walking out of here." His icy look froze her to the spot. "Sit *down*."

She sat again, feeling a bit like a marionette on strings, and wishing she were anywhere but here with these two people. A funeral. Even the dentist.

Or the gynecologist, with her feet in stirrups, and an

apologetic doctor holding a speculum between her thighs going, "*Sorry, but this will be cold and uncomfortable.*"

Literally. *Anywhere* else.

Mrs. Gale sniffed, crinkled her nose as if she smelled something foul, and crossed her arms. "How dare you bring one of your paramours into the company as an employee. What would your father say?"

She stiffened, every nerve within her screaming for her to tell this pompous woman exactly where she could stick her old-fashioned attitude. She stood again, nails digging into her palms. "You know what? You can take your—"

"Father would say nothing." He smoothly stepped in front of her and cut her off, all without even glancing her way. "We were working and had a dinner break together. We were both fully clothed, and she just happened to be under the table. That's it."

Mrs. Gale cast a glance at the table in question. "Oh, dear me. I didn't realize that wine at a business meal was now standard. Shall we serve that all day long at the break station, instead of coffee and tea? Perhaps throw in a few hard spirits, as well, to liven up the day? Some leftover medication that didn't pass FDA approval?"

Maggie's nails dug even deeper into her palms, but she miraculously managed to keep her mouth shut. She had a suspicion that this had nothing to do with her at all, and everything to do with *them*. Mrs. Gale was a force to be reckoned with. Word on the street was that she never stopped pushing till she got her way, no matter what stood in her path. Apparently, that ruthlessness extended to her son, so Maggie speaking up in his defense wouldn't do anything to help diffuse the situation.

If anything, it would only rile the monster even more.

Mr. Gale crossed his arms, not even close to losing his cool over his mother's...well, coolness. If anything, he looked mildly amused. The man was like a machine, all cold, hard logic and no irrational emotion at all. "That's not the same thing. It's after seven, and we're both finishing up a twelve-hour day on a Friday. Since my original dinner meeting was canceled, I invited Maggie to join me before I go home—*alone*, I might add. Not that it's any of your business."

"Then why was she under the table?" Mrs. Gale lifted her head and somehow managed to stare down her nose at her son, despite their height differences. "Let me guess. You were playing hide and seek. She seems to be of the age and intelligence level that she'd enjoy such trivialities."

Maggie gasped. "*Excuse* me. I graduated top of my class at—"

He interrupted with, "She dropped a fork and was picking it up."

"Ah, but no one will believe that." His mother shook her head. "Not once I tell the board the disgraceful behavior I witnessed. Interoffice relations are forbidden."

"Not always," he said, still looking completely bored.

If she had known she was going to get fired anyway, maybe she would have had a little bit of fun under that table first. Mr. Gale was an attractive man, and the way he'd been looking at her right before the interruption...

It had been scalding hot, to say the least.

Panty-dropping, to be more accurate.

Mrs. Gale snorted. "Well, unless the two of you were secretly dating before she came here, you don't have a leg to stand on. And you are well aware of it, too."

Maggie's boss looked at her, but remained silent.

It was almost as if he was asking her...no. *No.*

Surely he didn't mean...*no.*

"As I thought. She's fired, and that's that," his mother said, shooting Maggie a disdainful look. "It's time you stopped messing around with loose women, and did your duty as heir and primary share holder of Gale Incorporated. I set you up on a date with a lovely woman last night, and you didn't even show up, which is why I'm here in the first place. Do you know how long it took for me to smooth the waters with Sheldon?"

Maggie crept toward the door. Time to slink away.

He grabbed her hand, holding her in place.

"No, and I don't give a damn, either. I told you not to set me up with his daughter," Mr. Gale said, his voice clipped. "That's on you. You're the one who refuses to give up on the idea of me marrying some snob you handpicked for me."

"With good reason." His mother's nostrils flared. "I don't give up once I've decided on a course of action. It's a pity you didn't inherit my determination to win and stubbornness to be the best."

Maggie tried to discreetly wriggle free, not wanting to draw attention to herself, but failed. Her boss wasn't letting go. She glanced up at the ceiling. If ever a meteorite was going to swoop down on the city and kill her, now would be the perfect time.

"Funny that you think that. You tried to kick me out of this position," he pointed out, brow raised. "And yet here I stand. Holding steady."

"This is not a conversation for outsiders." She gestured to Maggie, her nose again scrunching up at the sight of their joined hands, as if she smelled the peasant on her. "Let her go. She's fired."

Mr. Gale shook his head. "No, she's not. And she's not going anywhere."

"Very well then. You want to dig yourself a deeper hole? Go ahead." She threw her hands up dramatically. "I'm through trying to protect you."

"*Protecting me*? When the hell have you ever—?"

"Language," his mother snapped, her face flushing. "You

listen, and you listen well, young man. You *will* go on the dates I set up for you, and you *will* do it with a smile on your face, and you *will* pick one of them to become your wife. It's what your father did before you, and your father's father, and your father's *father's* father. It is what's expected of you."

His jaw flexed, but he remained silent.

Apparently, Mrs. Gale wasn't finished yet. "You will be charming and every inch the gentleman *I* raised you to be. You will find a suitable woman to settle down with, and you will propose. Enough of these dalliances with low-class women—it's time to do your duty as heir and the head of this company. You wanted the position badly enough to fight me for it? You have it. Now it's time to take full responsibility for that position. It's been almost six years. It's time to be the man you're supposed to be. A man your father might possibly be proud of. If not, I swear, I'll—"

She cut herself off, *finally*.

Maggie, for one, was grateful for the silence.

Mr. Gale tightened his hold on her, but otherwise he showed no outward reaction to his mother's horrible words. Maggie tugged again, but to no avail. "Go on," he said. "Finish your threat. You've never held back before."

Mrs. Gale lifted her chin and pointed her haughty nose to the ceiling. "If not, I'll take this unfortunate situation to the board and use it to get you kicked out of your tenuous position as CEO of this company. Your brother is three years younger than you, and he's married a woman of suitable upbringing—"

"That you picked for him."

"Yes, that *I* picked for him," she said, stepping forward and pointing a manicured finger at his chest. "And they're married, with two little boys to carry on the good Gale name, as they should. They attend charity balls. He's every bit the CEO this company needs. If it were left up to you, you'd bring a lady of the night to the mayor's dinner next month."

Lady of the night? My God, what was this woman? Did she walk straight out of a Charles Dickens novel? Maggie lifted her chin. "If you're insinuating I'm—"

Mrs. Gale swung a glower on her that would scare the devil out of a hellhound. "I wasn't speaking to you."

She swallowed her words, staring back at the woman.

Where was that freaking meteorite?

Mr. Gale rocked back on his heels, finally showing some emotion. But it was amusement, not anger. "I wouldn't be the first to do so, and if you think otherwise, you're more naive than I ever imagined. Last week, Mr. Thorn brought a woman that I know for a fact is a—"

"*Don't.*" She dropped her hand and shook her head sadly, as if she'd caught him banging a woman in front of her late husband's shrine, instead of walking in on an awkward dinner between boss and employee. "You will announce an engagement before the next board meeting, or I will put forth a motion to remove you as CEO under a No Confidence vote, and do everything in my power to instate Andrew into the position in your stead. Don't make the mistake of thinking I won't get the votes needed. I will. I've ensured as much. As I said, I abhor losing."

He glanced at Maggie again, and the idea he'd planted with his silent gaze earlier took an insane, reckless turn. She'd been trying her best to ignore the plan forming silently in her head, but something inside of her snapped.

But she couldn't do it. Could she?

She didn't do things on impulse. *Ever.*

And yet, she was about to. Like a *boss.*

Ignoring her actual boss, she tossed her hair over her shoulder. "That's ridiculous, and this is the twenty-first century. You can't force someone to get married because you *want* them to."

Slowly, her boss turned to her, shock on his face as if he couldn't believe that someone was sticking up for him. Or maybe he'd forgotten she was there. Either way, it looked as if a strong gust of wind would have blown him right onto his perfect, tight butt. "Maggie—"

"Excuse me?" Mrs. Gale said. Her face flushed an angry red, and her hands fisted at her sides as she advanced on Maggie. "Who exactly are you to speak on this matter? And why are you still here? I fired you."

"Ah, but *he* didn't. And there's a reason for that."

Mr. Gale blinked at her, looking like a fish out of water for the first time.

His mother spluttered. "How *dare* you—"

"I'm your son's fiancée," she blurted out. "We were together before I joined the company. That's why he can't date other women, why he didn't show up last night. And it makes all of your threats empty ones, too. You can't fire me. So–yeah. He already wins, because he has *me*."

Mrs. Gale's jaw dropped. *Finally* the woman shut up.

But as quickly as her uncharacteristic impulsiveness had come into play, Maggie's common sense came right back. She'd literally just announced, without her boss's permission, that she was *engaged* to him. If he denied it in front of his mother, she would not only be fired, but everyone would hear about her shame, and no one would hire her.

New York might be a huge city, but the pharmaceutical research field was *not*.

And all of this had happened because she had a stupid soft spot for creatures who needed help. Her boss, with billions in his bank account, shouldn't fit into that category, but yet he somehow *did*.

Mr. Gale, who probably wanted to strangle her, choked and dragged his hands down his face. "Maggie, you don't—"

"It's okay. I told you I didn't want to announce it yet, but

I'm ready." She forced a smile. His mouth opened, closed, then pressed into a thin line. "We can tell the whole world how much we love each other if you want…Benjamin."

He made a strangled sound and tugged on his tie. He seemed more shocked than anything, but he had to be angry underneath that cold exterior of his. "Love—?"

She cast a quick glance at Mrs. Gale, who was starting to turn blue from lack of oxygen, before turning back to her boss. Not giving him a chance to ruin the ruse she'd thrown together, she launched herself into his arms and kissed him, right in his office in front of his mother.

The second their mouths touched, it was as if she'd woken up from a long, deep sleep. This wasn't a kiss—not really—and she was fully aware of that.

But her body didn't get the message.

His mouth softened under hers, and after a moment of sheer awkwardness, he closed his arms around her and hauled her against his chest. Though she'd initiated the kiss, it didn't take long for him to show her who was in charge of it. A small shift of his chin, and he was the *kisser* instead of the *kissed*.

He turned her slightly, facing away from his mother, and ran his tongue against the seam of her sealed lips. She gasped, shocked he'd actually gone *there*, and he took full advantage of the situation. He tasted like wine and something else she couldn't place, and that was about as far as she got before she couldn't think of anything except his lips on hers, his tongue against hers. She curled her hands into his shirt, and a small moan escaped her. She jumped at the sound, jerking back and covering her mouth in surprise.

Mr. Gale stared down at her, breathing heavily, his focus *clearly* on her mouth. It did weird things to her insides—things that made her want to launch herself back into his arms, only for real this time, and take that kiss a step further.

Like, stepping right into his bed.

She lifted her face, going for another taste. His eyes darkened, and a sexy growl escaped him, so quiet she might have imagined it. He fisted her shirt at the small of her back and closed the distance between them. She sucked in a breath.

If she didn't, she might pass out.

"*Enough*," Mrs. Gale shouted, forcibly jerking Maggie out of her lust-hazed tunnel vision. "If you think I'll buy this...this...*indecent sham* as something real, you're even less fit as the head of this company than I suspected."

Mr. Gale—God, she didn't even call him by his first name in her mind and she'd just *kissed* him—turned to his mother. Instead of letting her go like she'd expected, he tightened his grasp on her waist and kept her tucked against his side. "There's nothing indecent in this room. We love each other and aren't ashamed to show it."

"This is unacceptable. Whatever *this*"—she gestured between Maggie and Mr. Gale—"is, it needs to end. *Now.* I'll contact you with a list of suitable candidates, and you *will* woo them all. And you *will* pick one of them and kick *her* to the curb where she belongs...or you'll pay the ultimate price."

Not waiting for an answer, she stormed out, closing the door behind her with a firm click. Even though she hadn't slammed the door, the effect was still there. Maggie jumped and dropped her hand—which had been covering her mouth—to her side. Mr. Gale let go of her, and he immediately stepped back to a respectable distance.

She still didn't look at him. Didn't dare.

God, what had she *done*? So much for keeping her disastrous love life—real *or* fake—out of the office. She'd kissed her boss. Her *boss.* Jesus.

After counting to three, she blurted, "I'm sorry. So, so sorry, Mr. Gale. I have no idea what came over me, but she kept yelling and calling you worthless, and you work so hard and don't deserve to be treated that way, and I just, I don't know, *snapped*. I couldn't take it anymore, so I...I..."

"Did the perfect thing," he said, his voice as calm and collected as always. "Damn brilliant, really."

"It was stupid and irresponsible and—" She staggered back and glanced at her boss's face for the first time since they'd been left alone. "Wait. *What?*"

Instead of anger and disgust, which she'd totally expected to see, he smiled at her. Actually *smiled*. And he had dimples. Two of them. In his cheeks.

What just happened?

Chapter Three

Benjamin rubbed his jaw, and his smile widened as he replayed the look of pure shock on his mother's face when Maggie threw herself into his arms and declared their love for one another. *Love.* What a silly notion, and an absolutely perfect weapon against his mother's ultimatum. She would be as disoriented in the face of love as he would be, because neither of them had a clue what it was.

The Gale family ran on ambition, not *feelings*. And that was a damn good thing, too. If she had said they were marrying for money, or for convenience, his mother would have been on them quicker than a lion on a wounded gazelle.

But instead, she'd used *love.* It had been enough to send his mother running, and it had bought him some much-needed time to get his shit together. He had no doubt his mother could challenge his position if he refused to at least try to settle down and be responsible. But if he already had a fiancée…

Hell, she didn't have a case against him. And she was fully aware of that.

Maggie's ruse had literally saved him. Of course, she was panicking, and looked as if she might be close to running from the office. But after she handed him that ingenious plan, there was no way he was letting it slip out of his fingers. He'd make her see that it was resourceful, not irresponsible. Her lie saved both their asses.

They were in a win/win situation.

She licked her lips—lips that he couldn't get his mind off of now that he'd had a taste—and shook her head. "N-No. It was stupid. All she has to do is ask a few questions around the office, and she'll find out the truth. She'll fire me. I won't be able to pay my rent, or help my parents out back home. I'll be disgraced, and no one will hire me. I'll have to leave the city and go back to milking cows and training—"

Milking cows? Jesus. People still did that? Didn't they have machines for that? "Maggie." He pressed a finger to her soft lips, and she shut up. It took all his self-control not to kiss her into a silence, but he had a feeling if he did so, she'd bolt. She was already seconds from hyperventilating as it was. "It's okay. Everything's okay."

She flushed even more. "No, it's not. I messed up so bad, just like I always do, but this time it's at work."

"But we don't have to tell anyone. No one needs to find out." He lifted her chin with two gentle fingers, and her upturned face was more vulnerable than he'd ever seen it before, and so impossibly beautiful. He tried another smile, hoping to set her at ease, but if anything it seemed to freak her out even more—probably because he didn't smile much anymore. Or ever. "We can make this into something real. Well, not *real*, but for the sake of everyone else it will *look* authentic. Like we were dating all along."

Her gray eyes—they were definitely gray with blue flecks, now that he was this close to her—watched him, full of so many questions he could practically hear them. She was so different from the society women he usually dated.

The last one, Elizabeth, he'd been with for a year, and she never showed him even an ounce of emotion or softness. But Maggie? Ah, she showed every emotion as she experienced it, and it was refreshingly sweet. He didn't know how to do the same. All his life, he'd been trained to hide his feelings.

But she was so…so damn *open*.

A surge of protectiveness hit him. He'd do what it took to help her keep her job *and* to make her stay by his side. With her help, he could get to the bottom of his mother's plan. Hell, maybe he could talk to his brother and see if he was as eager for the position as his mother made him out to be.

He *would* win this battle.

But he'd need Maggie's help to get it done and to avoid endless dates with the insufferable, money-grubbing, empty-headed snobs his mother usually set him up with.

She stepped back, and he dropped his hand to his side. "No one will believe it. We're never alone together."

"Yeah, we are." He stepped closer, towering over her short height. She bit her lip and gave him a onceover. The air between them became charged, and he curled his fists into tight balls to keep from touching her again. "All the time. We always work later than everyone else, just like tonight. If we announce our engagement, people will all slap their thighs and go, '*That's* why they always stayed late.'"

She shook her head once. "It can't possibly be that easy."

"The hell it can't. People are gullible. Show them what they expect to see, and they believe it. If we tell them we stayed behind late to hide our *love* from the world, they'll eat it up." He paced, unable to stand still with so many ideas running through his head. "My mother will fall for it, too, since she already saw us on a date."

She spluttered. "It wasn't a *date*."

"I know that, and so do you." He pointed at her. "But she

doesn't."

She tugged on her fingers. "Okay, fine. Whatever. But why would you *want* to pretend to be engaged to me?" she asked, watching him as he paced back and forth. "I don't get it."

"You're the one who told her we were engaged in the first place," he said. "Not me."

"I know. And again, sorry. I'm never impulsive like that. I have no idea what came over me. I guess I just wanted to help you."

"I'm not impulsive either, and I *always* think things through. To the point of exhaustion, even." He stopped in front of her. "But *I* can see the merit of us pretending to be engaged, and you should be able to as well."

She pressed her mouth into a tight line. "And that is?"

"Well, for starters, you could be fired if she went to the board with what she 'saw' here tonight—and she does have that power, if she can convince them."

She paled. "She does?"

"Yes. It's against company policy, so we could both be punished. It would help her force me out as CEO, and you would be fired on the spot." He rubbed his jaw. "But with your smart lie, we wouldn't have to worry about it. If we act as if we're in love, and have been for a long time, we'll both be safe."

"That's great and all, but we'll have to convince people we're in a relationship." She held her hands out, palms up. "How do we do that?"

He'd seen it in movies, so it couldn't be that hard. Smile a lot. Kiss a lot. Hold hands. Stare into each other's eyes meaningfully. *I can handle that.*

"We act happy, just like regular couples do. Kiss. Smile. Date. Instagram how in love we both are, and how we can't wait to get married." He shrugged. "And then, after a suitable amount of time, we break up and continue on as we have been."

She shook her head. "But we have to pretend to be in *love*? That's *crazy*. Isn't it?"

"Maybe. Maybe not." He shrugged, his heart pumping hard and fast. "Either way, I think it's our best option. This way, you keep your job and I keep mine. No cow-milking necessary."

A small laugh escaped her. "But we'd have to actually, you know, *date*."

"Yeah." Another shrug. "And?"

"And...and you know nothing about me," she said, wringing her hands. "Nothing at all."

"That's not true. Remember when we worked on the Collins project for a week, and on Friday, it all fell apart?"

She blinked at him. "Yeah."

"We thought it was hopeless, that we'd end up failing the client because we didn't have the numbers or the presentation ready." He rested a hand on her shoulder and stared into her gorgeous eyes. She shivered and swayed closer. "We worked all throughout the weekend, only breaking for sleep, but we ended up giving them the best damn presentation we've ever given."

"You're saying this to prove we work well together, right?"

"Yep." He let go of her because if he didn't, and if she kept staring up at him, he wouldn't be able to keep his hands to himself. "And there's no way in hell you can argue with that."

"You're right. I can't. But you still know next to nothing about me."

"Sure I do. You're kind, smart, and think fast on your feet." He shrugged. "I can count on you to get a job done, and you're a loyal employee. If that's not enough for me to decide we make a good team, there's the fact that I enjoy working with you."

He purposely left off mentioning he liked *her*, because the appreciation he had for her had grown even stronger after her lie. Never in his life had anyone cared enough to try to help him like that. When his father died, and he'd been in a dark abyss of grief and shame, all his friends had abandoned him the second it became clear he wouldn't be paying for their drinks anymore. He'd been alone, struggling with guilt, for almost six years now.

And she'd jumped to his defense, like no one else ever had, tying them to each other in unexpected ways. His mother was every bit as ruthless as she let on. If she wanted to get Maggie fired, she would. Unless he did something. Unless he saved her. And he *would*. If there was one thing he'd inherited from his mother, it was her ruthlessness.

She took her turn at pacing, with short, agitated steps. Pressing her thumb against her mouth, she nibbled on the nail, clearly upset. It was so strange to be able to read her so easily, since he lived in a world of masks and fake smiles. "But we have next to nothing in common. Your family is as different from mine as night is from day."

"Night and day aren't that different, when you think about it. Both are ruled by a bright, round object in the sky. And both end in order for the other to begin." He stepped into her path, stopping her pacing, and caught her arms gently. Her skin was soft under his hold, and when she glanced up at him, every nerve in his body focused on her. "It's all about teamwork. And I, for one, think we'd make an excellent team."

"But—" She rested her hands on his chest then quickly jerked them back, leaving behind a searing heat. "Sorry. So sorry."

If there was one thing she didn't need to apologize for,

it was touching him. Every small caress, every soft stroke, reminded him what it was to be alive, instead of just living. And he didn't want to let that go yet. "I'll pay you," he blurted out. "Twenty thousand dollars."

"Wha—?" She choked on nothing, falling into a coughing fit.

"Thirty."

She coughed even harder, wheezing.

He patted her back, and by the time she was able to breathe again, he was prepared to pay even more, if that was what it took to get her to agree to be his fiancée. He'd never been so certain of anything in his life as he was of this. It wouldn't even be hard to pretend he'd fallen for Maggie. He looked forward to having an excuse to spend time with her. For all intents and purposes, he'd be her...*lover*.

He would be expected to kiss her. Hold her. Touch her. That was enough to make pretending to feel that foreign emotion called "love" well worth it.

She finally recovered from her surprise, shaking her head. He opened his mouth to up his offer, but she beat him to it. "I can't–*won't*—take money from you to continue a lie that *I* initiated in the first place," she finally said, her brow creased in a scowl. "You insult me by insinuating I would."

What? No one ever turned down his money. *Ever.* He scratched his head, not sure where to go from here. "But—"

"*No.*" She shook her head furiously. "Absolutely not."

He dragged his hands down his face, not sure how to deal with someone who wasn't out to profit from the situation. If she didn't want his money, what could he offer her?

Nothing. That's what.

He eyed her, trying to get a read but failing. "What will it take to get you to agree, then?"

"Not money," she spat, crossing her arms. "You can't *buy* me."

He held his hands up. "Okay, I'm sorry. I didn't mean to... I'm used to... Most people wouldn't turn down money. Actually, most people would have asked for more before 'reluctantly' agreeing."

"Then you obviously hang out with the wrong people." She shook her head. "And that's just sad."

Sad? *Maybe.* But he didn't give a damn about any of them, and they didn't give a shit about him. So he certainly wouldn't lose any sleep over it. "I said this before, but we make a good team, Maggie."

"We do," she said softly. "That's exactly what I'm scared of, because I don't want to mess that up, like I inevitably would. Pretending to love someone—"

That wasn't the first time she mentioned "messing up" in the area of her private life. "Let me guess. You and love don't get along?"

She blinked. "No."

"Well, I wouldn't recognize love if cupid shot me with a heart-tipped arrow straight through the chest. So we're the perfect match. Neither of us will get attached, because we both have no interest in doing so, therefore no one will get hurt." He caught her chin again, tilting her face up to his. "Please do this for me? For us?"

She locked eyes with him, swaying closer. The magnetism between them was undeniable, and he was getting pulled under her spell again. His blood rushed through his veins, heading down south to his already hard cock. Her pink lips called to him, beckoning him to take another taste. This time, nothing would stop him from taking it.

They might be talking about pretending to be a couple, but the attraction between them was one hundred percent real, so maybe he was going about this wrong. Instead of trying to buy her help, maybe he should try a sweeter path. He lowered his face to hers, slow inch by slow inch, and stopped just short of kissing her. "Maggie."

She gasped, her hands creeping up to grasp his shirt at his shoulders. "Mr. Gale—"

"Benjamin." He brushed his mouth across hers in a brief imitation of a kiss, and she tasted as sweet as he remembered. He watched her for any signs of rejection or hesitation, but she melted into him, letting out a small breath. "Call me Benjamin."

"Benjamin…if we do this, it has to be a business arrangement. It has to be clear-cut and easy. Pretend." Despite her words, she tipped her face up to his. "If we don't keep everything fake —it'll blow up in our faces. Trust me."

If we do this. That was all he heard out of that whole speech, because that meant she was considering it. He tasted victory, and it was as sweet as she was. "Deal. But we need to be comfortable with one another, too. To sell the whole 'in love' thing."

She nodded. "R-Right."

"So little kisses like this…" He brushed his lips against hers again and slid his hand down the curve of her hip, tracing the side of that hot little ass he'd done his best to ignore for the past six months. He moved closer, letting her feel exactly how much he wanted her—because there was no hiding *that* from her. "They have to come as easy to us as breathing."

She grasped his shoulders. "Mr. *Gale*."

"Maggie." He skimmed his hand around her waist, dipping down to tease the waistband of her skirt. He wanted to feel the soft skin there, to stroke it, but she had her shirt tucked in, and he couldn't cross that line. "You have to call me Benjamin."

"*Benjamin*."

"There you go." He chuckled and ran the back of his knuckles over her cheek. "That's not so hard, is it?"

Her gaze flitted down. "I don't know. Is it?"

A laugh escaped him. An actual *laugh*.

He'd spent years with his sights set on one goal only: to succeed as CEO. He'd been living, yes, but with her in his arms, he felt alive for the first time since his father's death. "I'll be honest, I've thought of doing this before. Touching you. And now here we are."

"Yeah." She nodded her head imperceptibly. "Here we are."

"What do you think?" He splayed his hand across her lower back, his pinky on the sweet curve of her ass, and the pulse at the base of her throat leaped. He pressed a soft kiss there, relishing her reaction to him. "Can we make this thing between us work?"

"If we're being honest, I definitely feel the attraction, too. That's why if we get caught up in the lie, it would be catastrophic."

Would. Not *could*.

Something told him Maggie had been hurt pretty badly before. That's what made her cautious about love, while he simply didn't understand the point of such a vulnerable emotion. It only led to pain. "But it could be really good, too."

She pulled him closer, her words at war with her actions. "If we do this, we shouldn't be doing"—she motioned between them—"this."

Despite her words, she didn't let go of him. If anything, she held him tighter.

"I'm fine with that, if that's what you want. I'll never force you to do anything you don't want to do. You can walk out of here, tell me to go to hell, and I'll still fight for your job till I can't fight anymore." He let go of her, even though every muscle protested the loss. "Do you want to leave?"

She bit her lip, staring up at him, still holding him tight. "No."

"All right." His pulse surged. "So, back on topic, if we're

going to do this, we'll have to kiss fairly often, to make it real. We'll have to be comfortable enough with one another…" He slid his hands back into place and dropped a kiss on her lips again, pulling back right away. "To do things like this without hesitation."

She lifted her face to his, a small breath puffing out, and her lids dropped down. She looked so damn kissable and fit into his arms like a missing piece of himself. "All the time. Try it again."

He kissed her again, his lips lingering over hers. "Like that?"

"Mm hmm." Her eyes opened, and she took a deep breath. "This is all a horrible idea."

He stepped back and cocked a brow. "Do I sense a 'but' coming?"

"*But* I'll do it." Her lips quirked. "You're right—we are a good team. If anyone can make this look real, it's us."

Feelings he hadn't let himself experience in years hit him. Gratitude, satisfaction, victory, and excitement—they were all there. The urge to pick her up and swing her in a circle was a tangible thing, but he didn't move. The man he used to be? He'd have done it. But the man he'd become wouldn't. Couldn't.

"Thank you, Maggie." He held his hand out for her to shake, even though he would rather kiss her. "You won't regret this. I promise."

She shivered and slid her hand into his, her gaze dipping to his mouth as she stepped closer. "Let's kiss on it. Make it official. That way we get more practice, and we get more comfortable—"

"You don't have to sell me on the idea." He hauled her into his arms and dropped a kiss perilously close to her lips. She gasped and rested her hands on his chest. "You want me to kiss you? I'll damn well kiss you."

He nibbled on her ear gently this time.

"G-Good. But we need to lay out rules, and times where I have to be seen with you, and—" He bit her ear a little harder, then sucked on it to ease the sting. She even tasted sweet there. Like cotton candy, but more addictive. And he fucking loved that fluffy, sugary shit. "*Benjamin.*"

Releasing the lobe he'd bitten, he kissed the side of her neck again, flicking his tongue over the sensitive skin there. He was coming on strong, but she kept making sexy little sounds every time he touched her, and he couldn't help it. "Was that too much?"

Her resistance faded with each brush of his lips on her soft skin, and the undisputable attraction between them was drawn so tightly it should snap. "Um, maybe…"

"I'm sorry." He brushed his lips across hers again, ever so slightly, lingering this time. "Just practicing."

"Yeah. Sure." She moaned and grabbed hold of him, swaying closer. "Practice."

Another almost-kiss had frustration boiling inside him because she hadn't showed nearly as much desire for him as he had for her. He didn't like wanting someone so strongly in the first place, but he'd be damned if it was one-sided. "Maggie—"

"Enough." She threaded her fingers through his hair and tugged hard, finally seeming to break. "*Kiss me.*"

I thought you'd never ask.

He closed the tiny distance between them, their lips melding together on one jointly exhaled breath. She melted against him instantly, her soft body curving perfectly into his. She fit against him as if she was made for him alone, and he had the sinking suspicion that she was. And that *terrified* him. He swallowed the impending sense of doom creeping up his spine, hauled her even closer, and deepened the kiss.

Again, she opened for him, and he kissed her like a

starving man. Never had he had something as sweet, or addictive, as Maggie Donovan. Pretending to love her would be a pleasure if it meant he got to kiss her. Hold her. Touch her.

Make her scream out his name.

Backing her against the wall, he gave her a second to push him away. When she didn't, he explored her body fully. She was all softness and curves, easily the most perfect combination of hotness he'd ever had in his arms. Instead of the toned, almost boyish frame of most of the women he'd dated, she was all curves, swells, and lean legs.

All *woman*.

Closing his palms over her large breasts, he ran his thumbs over her hard, perky nipples, cursing the clothing that stood in his way. At the slight pressure, she gasped and pressed against him wantonly. Her pencil skirt was in the way so he lifted it, inch by inch, so he could press his knee against her core. She gasped and dug her nails into his forearms, rotating her hips in a circle.

Her hands drifted up his arms, clinging to his biceps. A small, breathy moan escaped her. He swallowed her sounds of pleasure and increased the pressure of his knee, gaining a small cry from her lips. Her entire body tensed, and she moved against him, almost pushing away, but then pulling him closer instead. She rode his leg with a wildness he'd never seen before.

It made him even hotter to have her, *naked*, in his bed.

To make her his for real.

She rubbed herself against him frantically, her tongue swirling over his, and *bam*. She came, her whole body freezing as a tiny little whimper escaped, long and drawn out until it ended in a sigh. He could have kept going. Could have bent her over, and fucked her until she'd forgotten all about ever wanting to keep their relationship professional. But that wouldn't be fair. So, despite every single muscle in his body screaming for him to finish what he'd started, he let go of her and backed off.

Gave her room to breathe.

"Holy crap." She collapsed against the wall. "I never...I mean... Oh my God."

Smoothing her hair off her face and away from her swollen lips, he locked eyes with her. He shifted his position, trying to ease the throbbing insistence of his aching cock. She might have gotten more than a kiss, but he hadn't, and his body was all too aware of that fact. "Maggie..."

She licked her lips and shrugged off his hold, and he watched the wet path her tongue left behind, unable to glance away. "I need...I need a minute."

"Yeah. Sure." Pushing away from the wall, and her, he forced his expression into a cool, calm, collected mask. He had a hell of a lot of practice at doing so, but still it was harder than normal, which probably wasn't a good sign of things to come. "We should discuss rules and plans."

She tucked her hair behind her ear with a shaking hand and walked toward the door on trembling legs. She stumbled and he reached out to steady her, but she caught herself on the edge of his desk. "Yes, we should, but not now. I-I need to go."

"Okay." So he kissed her, and she bolted. His earlier suspicions had been confirmed—she was a runner. He'd scared her. Shaken her. Well, she'd shaken him, too. So they were even. "Meet me for dinner tomorrow? So we can discuss everything in detail?"

She froze in the doorway. "Where?"

"Macaluso's. Eight."

She hesitated, but nodded. "See you there."

He watched her leave, an emptiness taking hold of the pit of his stomach as she walked away from him, but it wasn't strong enough to dispel the satisfaction of having a plan in place. One that would secure his position, once and for all— while giving him an excuse to kiss Maggie.

As soon as the door shut behind her, he went into his private bathroom, locked the door, and undid his pants. Gripping the counter with his left hand, he closed out the world, a small smile slipping into place as he slid his right hand inside his pants, squeezing his erection. She was honest, fresh, sweet, and even better? Naughty as hell underneath those knee length pencil skirts and soft silk blouses.

He moved his hand faster, grunting as the pleasure made his balls tighten and pull up close to his body. The more frantically his hand moved, the more he pictured Maggie's face as she came, and how she'd ridden his leg—until, letting out a long groan, he came, hard and fast. It wasn't enough.

It wouldn't be until he had Maggie in his arms again.

Chapter Four

The next night, Maggie couldn't shake the feeling that she'd made a big mistake when she'd agreed to be her boss's fake fiancée. This whole thing was a horrible, terrible, no good, very bad idea. Ever since she'd agreed to pretend to be Mr. Gale's fiancée, nothing had gone her way.

From the moment she'd woken up that morning to her eventful trip to the restaurant to meet Mr. Gale, it had been a day from *hell*. While she wasn't exactly the superstitious type who read tea leaves or life lines on her palm, she couldn't help but think it was an omen of things to come.

And it might be best to listen.

Even so. Here she was.

Being an idiot, yet again, over Benjamin Gale III.

She'd spent the day getting "made over" by her roommate and best friend, Becca, and the result had been quite stunning…even if she'd been burned by the curling iron three times to achieve it. She wore a light gold dress that looked as if it belonged in a ballroom instead of some fancy restaurant, and her heels were sky high. High enough to hurt her ankles and make her wobble unsteadily every now and then, but the pain was totally worth it. Her hair had been swept into a loose side braid, and she couldn't help but feel like a princess.

She pulled out her phone. *I'm almost there. Wish me luck.*

You don't need it. Becca replied quickly.

Maggie looked out the window. They were almost there. *Are you going out?*

Nope. I have a hot date with Netflix and a bottle of wine.

Wish I did, too. Maggie blew out a breath.

Becca didn't reply back.

The cab she'd hired stopped outside a fancy restaurant that she'd never have set foot in on her own. A plate here cost the equivalent of a month's worth of groceries for her. Luckily, she wouldn't be paying. Her freaking rich *fiancé* would.

A hysterical laugh bubbled in her throat, choking her.

"Oh, God," she said out loud. "What were you *thinking*?"

She'd lied, and she'd have to deal with the consequences. Next time she wanted to swoop in and help someone out... she'd keep her stupid mouth shut.

No matter how hot the guy was.

Or how great a kisser.

Her stomach tightened when she remembered the way he'd made her combust in his office. She'd never, *ever*, come so hard, so fast, before. The way he touched her had made her whole body come to life, begging for more. It was all she'd been able to think about. But whatever. She'd be fine.

It wasn't as if she needed another taste. Or even wanted one.

God, even *she* snorted at that bold lie.

Yesterday, after his knee brought her to heights she'd never seen, she'd been a quivering mess. Benjamin had stepped back, watching her with cool detachment. That had been the worst part about that mind-numbing kiss. Sure, he'd said all those things about them being a good team, and working together was a pleasure, *blah blah blah*, but his tone had been cool. Aloof. Uninterested.

Completely unreadable.

Just like him.

After taking a long, deep breath, she paid the cabbie and opened the door. She'd go in there, they would plot their strategy just like they did in a normal business meeting, and she would treat it like any other day in the office. That was the secret. It would be fine. Everything would be fine. As soon as she—

She stepped out and landed her best pair of heels in a big, dirty puddle of questionable origins. "Oh, *come on*."

The cabbie turned in his seat. "There a problem?"

"No. It's nothing."

As she climbed from the cab, she smacked her head on the top of the car. This time she didn't even bother to cry out, because she wasn't even in the least bit surprised. It was just the way the day had been going. And would continue to go, from all appearances. She shut the cab door, and it pulled away...

Two seconds after she realized she'd left her purse in the backseat.

"Wait!" she screamed, raising her arm and chasing after him.

He stopped, and she managed to retrieve her purse in the nick of time. Hugging it to her chest, she closed her eyes and took a second.

Because, God, she *needed* a second.

"Come on, Maggie. You can do this. You're not cursed, and it's not an omen. Go in there, and it'll be fine. It's just another job."

"You weren't kidding, were you?" a slightly amused voice asked. "You really do like talking to yourself."

She shook her head and wished the sidewalk would just open up and swallow her, since that freaking meteorite had been a no-show last night. It would be better than whatever was coming next. "Sir?"

"Benjamin. You have to call me *Benjamin*." He walked up to her, and his woodsy, male scent washed over her. She breathed it in like it had healing properties. "Look at me, Maggie."

She did.

But she immediately wished she hadn't.

His blue eyes were locked on her, and his five o'clock shadow begged to be touched. His wavy hair curled to perfection next to sharp cheekbones that belonged on a statue of a Greek god, not a mere man. And his eyes...they were cold. Rock hard. "Everything will be fine. We're a good team, remember?"

"Yeah." She took a deep breath. "I know."

"I'm glad." Funny, he didn't *look* glad. "In this relationship, you're the boss, not me. It's only fair, since I'm the boss in the office. What you want, you get. What you don't want, you don't get. I want you to be one hundred percent happy. I don't want you to feel trapped, or taken advantage of. Not with me."

She just stared at him.

He kept saying nice things, but never seemed to actually care.

And she didn't think that was an *act*. Did he feel *anything* around her? Okay, he felt *something*, because she'd gotten up close and personal with his impressive erection last night, but how could he just shut it off like that? How did he remain so cold, all the time?

When she remained silent, he cleared his throat. "You look gorgeous, by the way. Simply stunning." Her stomach hollowed out, because the coldness in his eyes gave way to a heat that burned through her dress, leaving her bare. Even though he was only looking, it was if he'd touched her. *Everywhere.* "You're a true beauty. The kind that no amount of makeup will ever recreate."

Her whole body flushed. Yep. Everywhere. "I feel like Belle from *Beauty and the Beast.*"

"How fitting." He cocked his brow. "I guess that makes me the Beast?"

"If the shoe fits…"

He skimmed his gaze over her again, almost possessively. Didn't he *know* how much that made her tremble? He rested his hand across her lower back, dangerously close to touching her butt, and she pressed her thighs together. "Oh, it fits."

Just three little words. Nothing racy or scandalous. Even so, it made her want to throw herself into his arms and beg him to take her again. *God, he was good.*

"Benjamin." If he showed the slightest sign of burning desire for her right now, she had no doubt she'd be combusting on Forty-fourth Street. And that wouldn't work. "Another rule: You should save the intimate touching for when people are watching."

"There are tons of people outside," he deadpanned, running his thumb over her lower lip. "Doesn't that count?"

Yes. It totally does. Kiss me again. "No."

"All right." He stepped back and let go of her, like she'd asked. "Like I said, you're the boss. If you want me to keep my hands to myself, I will."

She didn't *want* him to. She *needed* him to.

She had a feeling if he didn't, she'd forget all about this being pretend. She'd fall for him, and he'd hurt her, just like all the other men in her life had. She'd end up quitting her job anyway, and this pretense would have been for nothing. "I do."

"All right." He inclined his head and offered her his arm,

hardly looking brokenhearted over her rejection. "Ready to go inside? Or do you need to continue your little pep talk to yourself first?"

"I'm good, thank you," she managed to say with her head held high. Her cheeks, though, were on fire. "I'd just finished when you came up to me."

She slid her hand into the crook of his arm, and he hugged it close to his hard side. Just that slight contact made her legs shake. The man was made of pure, lean muscle. When did he have time to work out? He spent all day and most of the nights in his office. "I find it charming, you know. The way you talk to yourself."

Oh, she doubted that. Especially since he'd said those words without a hint of a smile. But she'd humor him anyway. "Thanks."

They walked inside Macaluso's, and as soon as he set foot on the threshold, it was as if the restaurant *knew* it. Waiters bowed and scooted out of the way, greeting him by name, and he led them to a small, private room in the back left corner of the dining room without any help. It was ensconced within dark red curtains, and there were at least ten candles flickering on random tables…

That were all empty of place settings except one.

He led her to that table, pulled her chair out for her, and waited. "Maggie?"

"Uh—" She blinked. "Is this whole room for us?"

"Yes." His brow wrinkled, and he looked confused, as if he didn't realize that most men didn't do that. How… How…*ridiculous.* "I don't want anyone overhearing our conversation. I wouldn't put it past my mother to have spies following us, to see if we're the real thing or not."

"Oh. Right." That, at least, sort of made sense. She sat down, and he pushed her chair in close. "Thanks. After the day I've had, I can't wait to get an appletini. Or five."

Anything to make her forget all about *this*.

And that sexy kiss last night.

He sat across from her and picked up a dark, expensive looking bottle of wine she'd somehow missed sitting in an ice bath. "No need to wait for a drink. I pre-ordered our wine to go with our meal. This is their best bottle of white."

I hate white. She smiled anyway because booze was booze, and at this point, she'd take it. She'd drink muddy water if it dulled the panic rising inside her with each word he said. Now that they were out, alone, the enormity of what she'd agreed to hit her. This was her *boss,* and she was on a *date* with him because she was pretending to be his lover. *How had this happened?* "Uh...thanks. Sure."

"Oh." He brandished a bouquet of red roses from under the table like some sort of hot, designer-suit-wearing magician. "Also, some flowers for you."

He said that with no emotion whatsoever, as if he could do this in his sleep. She had the impression he *was*, right now. "Thanks." She lifted the tablecloth and glanced underneath. "What else do you have under there? A waiter? A string quartet with a violin?"

His lips twitched, but he didn't smile. Heaven forbid he show some small sign of amusement. "No, they'll come in later."

"Seriously?"

A slight tip of his head. "No."

"Thank God," she breathed.

This whole "date" thing was so cliché. And more than likely? It worked every freaking time. This was obviously his play when he took women out, and he had all the right moves to make a normal girl swoon and fall into his arms. Unfortunately for him, she wasn't a normal girl, and she knew a well-honed player move when she saw one.

It wouldn't work on her.

She'd learned her lesson the hard way. Not that it mattered, of course. He didn't *have* to woo her. She was already his fiancée.

Laughing lightly at that, she took the flowers and set them on the empty table next to them without smelling them. She was well aware what roses smelled like, and they made her sneeze. She preferred snowbells. "Pretty flowers. Thanks."

"You're welcome."

She smiled, not saying anything else.

His forehead scrunched, and he scratched his head.

He seemed confused, and she almost felt sorry for him. He obviously couldn't figure out why she wasn't swooning at his feet. But the risk outweighed the reward, and she couldn't afford to be an idiot over her boss's dreamy eyes. Her job was too important. Her parents counted on her to help them, and her rent had to be paid, and poor Lucifer needed that vet appointment.

So he could turn those sexy eyes elsewhere.

He poured a full glass of wine, and held it out to her. Their fingers brushed on the hand off, and the skin on skin contact sent her pulse soaring and her mind racing back to that kiss for the millionth time. Seemingly unaware of her reaction to him, he settled in to pour his own glass. Before he'd even finished, she'd taken a big gulp. It tasted awful.

It might be their best bottle of white, but it still tasted like butt.

She must have made a face, because he sighed and set the bottle down. "What's wrong?" he asked, his voice tinged with slight annoyance.

"Nothing." She folded her hands in her lap and smiled, trying to ignore all the unsettled feelings swirling in the pit of her stomach. "Why do you ask?"

"You're acting strange."

Did that mean she wasn't acting like the million other

women he'd practiced his way too smooth moves on? "Lucky for you, this date is all for show, and you don't need to worry about what I'm thinking."

He downed some of his wine and tugged on his tie. The waiter came in carrying salads—wait, they hadn't even *ordered anything*—and set them in front of them. She took the opportunity to check him out since he was talking to the waiter.

He, of course, was as devilishly hot as always.

Benjamin—not the waiter.

He wore a black suit, a light blue shirt, and a gray-and-blue striped tie. He seemed to like stripes—probably because they were even and never out of place. His jacket hugged his body perfectly, since it had clearly been custom made for him. Guys like him didn't buy off the rack. That would never change. He came across as every inch the gentleman accustomed to such a lavish lifestyle…

While she felt like a little kid playing dress up, hoping her mother wouldn't come in and catch her wearing her favorite pearls before she could put them back where they belonged. And that was something that would never change, either.

Their two worlds just didn't make sense when put together.

The waiter bowed and left without even speaking to Maggie, or leaving a menu behind for them to read. She glanced down at her salad. It had blue cheese dressing on it.

Moldy cheese. Yum.

She pushed it away and set her hands back in her lap, linking her fingers together. "When will they bring the menus?"

"I already ordered us both their finest," he answered dismissively, looking devilishly handsome as he picked up his fork. How the man managed to make a freaking fork look sexy? She had no idea. But he did. "They'll bring the courses in when we're ready for them."

Oh. My. God. He really had this whole thing down pat.

"Excellent," she said drily. "Can't wait to see what I'm eating tonight."

He set his fork down and sighed again. "You're displeased."

"No. It's just that this isn't going exactly how I expected it would." She smiled and downed the last of her wine. "More wine, please?"

He poured her more and lifted a finger. A waiter brought another bottle within seconds. It was on the tip of her tongue to ask the man for an appletini instead, but he left as quickly as he came, yet again without even glancing at her. She rolled her eyes at the slight, picked up her wine, and drank some more. It would go straight to her head on her empty stomach, but she was past the point of caring.

At this point, she'd do anything to get through this evening without telling her boss that he sucked at first dates. Because he did. Horribly.

Too bad he didn't suck at kissing, too.

It would make resisting him *so* much easier.

Her stomach growled angrily, so she picked up a piece of bread and took a bite. That, at least, was delicious. "Mm. Good bread," she said, holding it up to Mr. Gale—*Benjamin*. "You should try some. Don't worry, I won't throw it at you this time."

He ate a bite of salad and watched her. Once he swallowed, he patted at his mouth with the linen napkin. "What's going on?"

Besides the fact that this was the most awkward date she'd ever been on? "Nothing." She picked up her glass of wine and took another sip, fighting back the cringe that tried to creep out. "I already told you that."

He leaned back, rested his elbows on the arms of the

chair, and let his hands cross in front of him. They fell silent. He sat there looking sexy, and she pushed her salad around on the plate. Sighing, he picked up that darn fork again and ate a few bites. After a while, though, he must've realized she hadn't actually eaten any of hers.

Frowning, he studied her with an intensity that sent goose bumps crawling over her skin. "You might think you're good at pretending you're all right, but I can read you like an open book, so I see you're not happy. Tell me what's wrong."

"Why do you care?" she asked softly. "What's it matter to you?"

"I didn't exactly say I did care," he replied, cocking his head. "I just said I could see it. But regardless of what you seem to think, I want you to enjoy yourself. I'm not that cruel."

Her heart thumped. "I am. Like I said, I'm fine."

"Good. In that case..." He reached into his pocket and pulled out a bright blue box. "I picked this up today."

She froze, and her stomach dropped to the floor with dread. She would have been more at ease if he'd slid a pair of padded handcuffs across the table. "Please tell me that's not what I think it is."

"It's a ring." He frowned and pushed the box closer to her. "If that's what you think it is, then, yes, you're correct."

Oh, God. She recognized the Tiffany & Co. box all too well. Every girl in America was fully aware what that bright blue color meant. But if he'd gone to Tiffany's, he'd spent a fortune on a fake fiancée, and she'd punch him in his stupid, perfect face.

And he'd deserve it.

She couldn't wear something like that on her finger. It probably cost more than she made in a year—or two. With her luck, she'd end up losing it and owing him a buttload of money when this was all said and done. And she couldn't afford that. So she rested her fingers on top of his, and pushed it right back to him, ignoring the way his skin felt against hers. "A fake engagement doesn't qualify for a real ring. Take it back."

"Actually..." He pushed the box closer to her again, his hand still under hers. "It does. My mother will notice if you're wearing a fake rock."

"You can't *tell.*"

He cocked a brow and didn't say a word.

He didn't need to.

"Oh, fine. Maybe *she* can." Maggie grabbed the box and flipped it open without looking at it, her heart racing. "But that doesn't mean I need a gaudy, huge—" The second she glanced down, the words died in her throat. The ring was gorgeous.

Of freaking course.

It wasn't obnoxious or gaudy at all. As a matter of fact, it was exactly what she'd want, if this engagement thing were for real. A simple princess cut diamond rested in the middle of a thin platinum band. It was huge, yes, but it was set elegantly, so it didn't look like too much. She swallowed and ran a hand across the stone.

"You were saying?" he asked, his tone tinged with amusement.

She didn't respond. Truth be told, she didn't think she was capable. He scooted out of his chair and took the box from her hand. She let him. He removed the ring and grabbed her left hand. "I wasn't sure about your size, so I made an educated guess with the help of the salesperson."

"What did you tell her?"

"Your height and approximate weight." His lips twitched into an almost smile. "Don't ask me to tell you what I told her. I know a trap when I see one."

She laughed, but cut it off quickly when he slid the ring into place. It was a little loose, but not uncomfortably so. His calloused fingertips scraped the back of her finger, and she swallowed hard. "You must've done pretty well. It fits."

"Good." He curled her hand into a fist and stared down at it. He kept touching her and making her body react to him in ways it shouldn't, but that wasn't what made her breath catch in her throat. For a second, as he stared at her, he looked almost...reverent. As if the sight of his ring on a woman's hand affected him in some way.

It affects me.

"It looks good on you."

She glanced down, her heart thumping loudly in her ears. He was right. It did. "Thanks. I...I love it. But I'll give it back after this is over."

"Keep it. Sell it. Whatever."

He dropped his hold on her and sat back in his chair. He looked about as moved as a sack of potatoes, so she must've imagined the earlier moment they'd shared.

She slid her hand into her lap and stole one more glance at it. "No way. It had to have cost a fortune."

"To be honest, I have no clue. I just handed her my card."

"*You just handed her—*" She spluttered, cutting herself off. He wouldn't understand why him dropping a small fortune on a ring for his fake fiancée, without even caring about the cost, was such a shock to her. "I mean...I see."

He rubbed his jaw, staring at her closely. "You're disappointed again."

"No. I'm just realizing how different we are."

He crossed his arms, watching her with a calculation that had her wanting to hide from his probing gaze. "And that's a bad thing?"

Yes. "No. But, I mean, this dress? It's not something I normally wear. I'm like a kid playing dress up, while you probably sleep in suits."

He didn't say anything at first, just observed her skeptically as she lifted her glass to her lips. "Actually, I sleep naked."

She choked on her wine. Legit choked.

A smirk slid into place on his face. A stupid, sexy one. He pulled something out of his pocket while she gasped for breath. "And as far as clothes go, we can buy you a new wardrobe. And lots of jewelry to go with that ring."

She covered her mouth, still gasping for air. "You—I— you shouldn't have said that."

"And yet, I did." He placed a Visa card in front of her. "Back on topic, before you complain or say it's too much, hear me out. I have lots of events to attend, and, as my fiancée, you'll be expected to be by my side. So there will be a need for dresses, and diamonds, and whatnot. Anything you need, you can just swipe my card, and it'll be yours."

Her pulse accelerated so steeply, it was a wonder she didn't fall over dead of a heart attack. "What do you mean? What events?"

"Let's see…there's the mayor's ball next Friday, and Saturday there's a gala at Rockefeller Center. Sunday's a matinee at the Richard Rodgers Theatre to benefit kids with cancer." He counted off on his fingers. "So this week alone, you'll need three dresses, and accessories, too. Don't skimp on the jewelry. No one will expect you to wear the same thing twice. It's unheard of."

Her heart raced even more, and she held the edge of the table, trying to ignore her fight or flight instinct kicking in. But this was it. This was how she was going to die. "I–"

"Do you speak French? Next week we have an event with the French Ambassador, and it would be awesome if you could—"

The waiter came in carrying two steaming entrées, so he stopped talking. Another server scurried in before him, taking the salads away with aplomb. The second the scent hit her nose, her throat closed up. He set down a huge plate of lobster tail—death on a dish for her. It was the last straw.

She scooted back, a hand to her throat, and stood.

Benjamin stood, too. "What? What is it?"

"I...I—" She shook her head, backed up slowly. "I can't do this."

"Maggie, wait!"

No way. Uh-Uh. No, sir.

She was *out* of there faster than a line drive out of the ballpark.

This whole date was a disaster, just as she'd expected. There was no way this could work. All the signs in the universe were telling her to run, and it was time she listened.

Before it was too late.

Chapter Five

Benjamin had no idea what the hell had spooked Maggie, but obviously *something* had. She'd been standoffish ever since he'd brought her into Macaluso's, and he'd been unable to figure out why. He'd treated her to the best of the best, and tried to do everything in his power to please her.

Instead, he'd pissed her off and *literally* sent her running.

And now he was stuck chasing after her.

He had a feeling this would be a running theme in their relationship—no pun intended. He caught up to her outside the restaurant because she'd stopped and was bent over, resting her palms on her thighs as she took a shuddering breath. "I can't. I can't do it. I can't—"

"Shh."

She jumped as if she was surprised he'd followed her. "Benjamin?"

Apparently, she'd been talking to herself again.

He crouched in front of her and cupped her cheeks, sliding his hands under her soft brown hair. She let him. Something tender, and almost calming, unfolded in his chest. As if she belonged there, with him, and he was only just realizing it—which was shit. She wasn't his. Not really.

This was all for pretend.

"Take a deep breath. In. Out." She did, staring at him the whole time, and that quietness inside him spread even more. "There you go. That's it. Now, slower this time." Maggie nodded and took another long inhale. She watched him with wide eyes, lips parted, and the trust in her eyes crashed into his chest, punching the air out of his lungs. "Good. Easy, now."

When her breathing settled into a more human pattern, mirroring his, she pulled away and swiped her hand across her forehead. He fought the urge to pull her back into his arms, where she belonged, damn it. "I'm sorry. I just...I'm allergic to shellfish. And when it was all there, in front of me, I couldn't *breathe*."

"Oh." *Shit.* He was a fucking dumb-ass. He'd been so intent on wooing her with fine wine and fancy meals, and waving his cash around, that he hadn't even stopped to consider she might not be able to eat what he'd ordered. Then again, he never did. This was just the first woman he cared to *get* to know better. He wanted to learn more about her—like what not to order if he didn't want to kill her. "I'm sorry. I didn't think."

She waved a hand dismissively. "You wouldn't have. I mean, you didn't ask me, so how could you have?"

Ah, so that was what was bothering her. She didn't like his take-charge attitude. But that was always how his dates went. He took charge. No one had ever minded, until now. "You wanted to be asked. That's what you're saying."

"Well, yeah." She blew out a breath, and her hair fluttered. "Of course I did. I'm not some empty-headed bimbo who can't order for herself what she wants to eat or drink."

He stared at her, trying to make sense of her actions

and words. She was so refreshingly different from the other women he'd dated, who looked to him to do everything, and he liked that about her. Being with her was a partnership. A new kind.

But it also made predicting her actions a lot harder than it should have been. And a hell of a lot more painful when he got it wrong, because he wanted to get it right. Because, damn it, he liked her. A *lot*. And, stupidly, he wanted her to like him, too.

Like he was back in grade school, or some corny-ass shit like that.

Nodding slowly, he took a deep breath. "Of course you're not. How stupid of me to treat you the way I did. Can you forgive me?"

She swallowed. "Benjamin..."

"I know," he said quickly, studying her. She looked a little less pale now. Her red lipstick was as flawlessly applied as before, and she was prettier than a real princess. She fit the part of the socialite so well that he'd forgotten she *wasn't* one, and he'd come on too strong. "I'm sorry. Next time, I'll ask."

She shook her head. "This...we...you want us to pretend to be in love, but how can we do that if we literally know *nothing* about each other? What would your mother say if she found out you ordered your fiancée a meal that would kill her?"

Damn it, she had a point. But they could work on that. "So, that's why you left the restaurant? The lobster? Not because you didn't want to be my fiancée?"

"No. God, no." She straightened and gripped her purse tight. "I don't want to do that, either."

"Good, because—" He froze, her words finally hitting him. His stomach twisted into a tight, mangled ball, and he shook his head. "Wait, what do you mean? You said you'd go through with it. You promised."

"That was before. Look, we're simply not a match. Fake or real, we'd never work. I'll never be able to sell this." She gestured between the two of them. "Sure, you're a good kisser, and you have a great knee, but that wouldn't be enough to make me love you, let alone marry you, in real life. And anyone who knows me would call me on it."

"We only need to convince people in my life, really, and—" He cut himself off. She'd said... He wasn't sure whether to laugh or be insulted. "I have a great *knee*? What the hell is that supposed to mean?"

"Nothing," she said. "But I don't like this whole alpha male thing you do. It would drive me insane in less than a week."

A muscle in his jaw twitched. The things this woman said... "What alpha *thing* do I have going?"

"You take women on dates, and throw your money at them to get them into your bed, and woo them with generic roses. I'm sure it works. I'm sure they all throw themselves at you." She crossed her arms and stepped back, shaking her head. "But I'm not them, and the waste, and the utter thoughtlessness behind the gestures...it's all empty. I can't do it, not even to save my job."

He held his arms out. "I take my dates to nice restaurants, order the best food and wine, and give them roses. Is that wrong?"

"No. But it's not *me*. And everyone who knows *me* knows that." She pressed a hand to her chest, which rose and fell rapidly. He didn't glance down, because he couldn't afford to be distracted right now. Too much was at stake. "Look, I want to help you. I do. But I can't pretend to be something I'm not. I don't speak French, and I don't want to buy a ton of diamonds, or eat with the French Ambassador, or the mayor. I didn't even *vote* for him."

"That's okay." He dropped his hands. "I didn't vote for

him, either."

She let out a small laugh and shook her head. The moonlight played with her hair, making it shine. Even when trying to run from him, she was the most beautiful woman he'd ever seen, and nothing would stop him from chasing her. "Okay, but still. I don't want money and credit cards and *all the things.*"

"I'm going to be honest. You confuse the hell out of me, Maggie," he said, reaching out to trail his knuckles down her cheek. "Most women I've dated would be pleased to get a credit card for unlimited spending, and jewels, too."

She shuddered, but didn't pull away. "Yeah, well, I'm not most women."

He crossed his arms, eyeing her with a new appreciation that had nothing to do with their fake relationship, or his need for her help. "I'm getting that now."

"You want a puppet you can dangle in front of your mother, who fits in with your crowd." Maggie twisted the ring on her finger and took it off, holding it out to him. "And I'm not that girl. I've never been good at fitting in, or falling into line, so chances are I'm not about to start now. Not even to keep my job, which I happen to enjoy a lot, for the record."

He didn't take the ring, but he pinched the bridge of his nose. "Maggie, I'm sorry I screwed up. I am." More than she'd ever understand. "Like I said, you're in charge. But I didn't know I was doing anything wrong. I just did what I always do when I take women out."

"You always give women Tiffany rings on the first date?"

He snorted. "No."

"And credit cards?"

He held up a hand. "You've made your point. It was too much, too fast. I won't make that mistake again."

Her lips twitched, and she seemed less inclined to run. "You think I'm a girl who's impressed with money, and jewels, and fancy restaurants."

"But you're not." He stepped closer, watching her for any more signs of her being ready to bolt. She looked steady, and he had to keep it that way. He couldn't afford to lose her. "Please, let me try again. And if you don't want to buy yourself diamonds...don't buy diamonds. If you want to wear a plastic bag to the galas, go for it. I don't give a damn, as long as you're there with me."

She bit her lip. "But what will everyone think?"

"Whatever they want to think." He moved into her personal space. "Who the hell cares?"

She eyed him and gestured toward the restaurant. "You do, I'd say."

"Nah." He tucked her soft hair behind her ear and skimmed his knuckles over the porcelain skin of her cheek again. He couldn't help it. Touching her was a drug, and he'd take his hits wherever and however he could. "I don't. I'm kind of a loner, so if they don't like me...I really don't give a damn."

She couldn't *actually* come to his galas in a bag, but he knew she wouldn't, so they'd be fine. She had more fashion sense than that. She just needed a minute to breathe. To accept it all. He'd had a lifetime to acclimate to a certain lifestyle. She'd had a *day*.

"Tell you what. How about this?" He tugged on her hair before letting go. It was harder to release that small piece of her than it should have been. "You pick the next 'date.' Show me what you like to do, so I'll know what to plan when it's my turn again."

She stepped a little closer, and he knew he had her. That she wasn't going anywhere. "When?"

"Whenever, and wherever, you'd like." He held his hand out to her. She didn't turn away. "Put the ring back on and give me one more chance."

She hesitated, but slipped the ring back onto her finger, and then slid her hand into his. "Okay."

He felt a surge of satisfaction that had nothing to do with tricking his mother into believing this was real. For whatever reason it might be—stubbornness, attraction, or something else entirely—he didn't want to let Maggie go.

Metaphorically or physically. But he did it anyway. He dropped his hold on her after one good shake. "Then it's set. How about we go back in, and you can order what you want this time?"

"I'd love that, Mister—" She cut off, smiling at him. And when she did that, the breath punched out of his chest again. "*Benjamin.*"

He'd never wanted to kiss someone so damn badly as he did Maggie, just then, under the full moon. If he curled his hand behind her neck, burying his fingers in her long brown hair, and slowly tugged her closer, would she fight him? Or would her gray eyes widen and her lips part in anticipation as he closed in on her mouth, one slow breath at a time?

A cab honked behind them, and he shook his head, shaking off the fantasy. She'd made it quite clear she didn't want to touch him unless absolutely necessary. "After you."

She went past him, leaving behind the tantalizing scent of flowers and vanilla. He followed her, doing his best not to stare at her swinging ass. But in that dress, it was impossible. It embraced her curves like a second skin, and she had to be aware of it. *He* sure as hell was.

As she sat down at their table, he picked up the plates of lobster, carried them to the waiter and whispered, "We need to start over, please. Bring the menus…and an…uh… appletini? Is that a real thing?"

The waiter bowed. "Yes, sir, it is."

"Great. Thank you." Benjamin straightened his jacket and walked over to the table, his heart beating in tandem with each step he took toward her. The more time he spent with her, the more he realized that, this game they played with one another? It wasn't in his control at all. And that was a sobering thought. He wasn't a man who relinquished control easily. "Our menus are coming."

She smiled at him, making those damn freckles of hers dance. "Excellent."

He settled into his seat and tugged on his jacket sleeves uncomfortably. It was hot as Hades in here. He'd give a leg to take the thing off, but he couldn't. She might not want a fancy first date, but he wasn't about to remove his jacket in a five-star restaurant.

And for the first time ever, he had no idea what to say to a woman. All his normal topics would fall flat with Maggie, just as his earlier tactics had. She unsettled him.

He wasn't sure how to feel about that yet.

"By the way…" She eyed the credit card in the middle of the table. "You can take that back now."

"You don't want it, but hear me out." He leaned in, and she did the same. The way she stared at him, all wide eyes and parted lips, tested his resolve to keep his hands to himself. "There truly will be a lot of events, and you'll need clothes of some sort to wear—it doesn't have to be designer, but you'll need *something*. Do you have a whole closet of ball gowns?"

She hesitated before shaking her head. "No."

"So take it. I don't want you struggling to buy dresses for events you're only attending because of me." He shrugged, but he could see he was already winning the argument. "Use it for emergencies when you have nothing that will work."

For a while, she didn't move. "I'll take it, but I'll only buy what I absolutely need to."

He nodded, taking the win.

It still baffled him that she'd refused money for her participation in the charade, and had actually been insulted at the mere suggestion. Maggie was an enigma he'd never unravel. She seemed too good to be real. In his life, when something presented as too good to be true—it usually wasn't. "Good."

"You said I'm the boss, but I don't want to be. I want this to be an equal partnership." She offered him a small smile. "Like a real relationship, basically."

Again, he nodded. "Deal. What else?"

She tapped her finger to her chin. "Let's see. We already covered the no kissing part…"

He held a hand up. "Until you ask me to, that is. Then that rule is out the damn window, where it belongs."

"That's not going happen, but I'll accept your terms, if that makes you feel better."

She'd lit up once they started talking rules. It was clear she liked setting up boundaries as much as he thought he'd enjoy crossing them. "I respect that, and I respect your clause about keeping things businesslike. Just like I appreciate your acceptance of my addendum." He lifted his glass in a toast to her. "Was that professional enough for you?"

She blinked at him, taken aback by something. He wasn't sure what, till he realized he was smiling again. When he was with her, it was a lot harder to hide the happy person he used to be, to keep the controlled, robotic appearance up at all times. Around her, he wanted to be himself, and…

It was a lot harder to act like his father.

He quickly erased the smile and cleared his throat, tugging on his tie again. She stared at his chest, swallowing hard. "Well? Are we good to go?"

"Yeah," she said, shifting in her seat and nibbling on her lip. "We're good."

They stared at one another, the tension between them building.

He swallowed a gulp of wine, set it down, and leaned

in again. She did the same. It would be so easy to close the distance between them and kiss her like they both wanted. But she wasn't ready, and he was a patient man. Even so, he couldn't resist saying, "Just for the record? I reserve the right to do my damnedest to change your mind about the no kissing thing, with every weapon in my arsenal, until you're begging me to fuck you."

Her nostrils flared, and she reared back, breathing heavily. She pressed a hand to her stomach. "Benjamin."

"And trust me." He settled into his chair and eyed her. "It's just a matter of time. Once I set my mind on something, I always win."

A nervous laugh escaped her. "Think what you want, but I never beg. And even if I did? I've already seen your moves, and they don't work on me."

He set his glass down. "Challenge accepted."

"Oh, hold up." She shook her head, looking more alive than he'd ever seen her. "I didn't lay down a challenge. I would never challenge a man like you."

"Sure you did. I heard it, loud and clear." The waiter came up behind her, carrying a frothy green concoction of a drink. "Ah. Here's your appletini, darling."

"My—? I didn't order one yet."

He lifted a shoulder. "Nope, but I did."

"But—" She glanced over her shoulder and then slowly turned back to him. "You remembered I said I wanted one?"

"I did." He reached out and covered her hand. It trembled beneath his, and she shifted her legs under the table, her knee brushing his. "From now on, I'll always remember what you tell me. I'll be waiting, planning, and finding your weaknesses, until you finally accept what I accepted the second you kissed me and called me yours—that we belong together, naked, in a bed."

She eyed him with a mixture of excitement, desire, and

wariness. It was a feeling he was all too familiar with, because it was exactly how she made *him* feel. After the drink was placed in front of her, she considered it with a small smile. "I underestimated you, Benjamin."

"That's okay. I did the same thing to you."

She tipped her head to the side. "But not anymore?"

"You bet your pretty little ass I won't do it again. Like I said, I plan on using every weapon I can against you, till I win." He casually entwined his fingers with hers as the waiter laid down their menus. It was absurd how fucking right it felt to hold her hand. After they were alone again, he waited until she lifted the glass to her lips and took a sip before he added, "Including my magical knee."

She snorted, which was unfortunate since she was in the process of swallowing. She inhaled the liquid, her face reddening as she set the drink down, coughing and cursing him in between breaths. "I. Will. Kill. You."

He laughed, pressing a hand to his stomach as she glowered at him and wiped her mouth. He killed the laugh off quickly, but he couldn't bring himself to regret the rare show of emotion. She stared at him as if he was a ghost, but he didn't care.

That had been way too much fun.

"Keep trying, if you wish, but no one else has succeeded yet."

"Oh, but I know things." She gripped the table with her free hand and waggled her brows. It didn't escape his notice that she hadn't pulled free of his touch yet. "Lots of things."

He cocked a brow and ran his thumb over the backs of her knuckles. "So do I."

She laughed and lifted her glass again, and he realized he'd smiled more in this short timespan with Maggie than he had all the rest of the night, while he tried to be what he thought she'd want him to be. Now that he was relaxing, and being himself instead of a shallow copy of his father...

It was actually fun. *Imagine that.*

"To winning?" she asked, holding up her glass.

"To *you* losing," he countered, clinking his to hers. "And us both being completely satisfied afterward."

"Careful, you might blow your load a little too early with all that false confidence."

He cocked a brow. "It's adorable that you think it's false. It really is."

"You keep chasing, I'll keep running." She lifted a shoulder. "You'll see who wins eventually."

Yeah. Him. But since he wanted her more than he'd wanted anything in his entire life, and she was determined to keep him at arm's length...

He probably should've let her keep running.

A few hours later, Benjamin had his driver stop the car in front of Maggie's home. He opened the car door and got out, offering her his hand. She held on tight as she slid out, steadying herself on her heels.

Once she was good to go, she let go of him quickly.

He let her.

"Thank you," he said, glancing down and adjusting his tie, "for giving me a second chance tonight."

She smiled and helped him, tugging slightly until it was straight. The small, kind gesture made his throat tighten and his pants shrink. "You're welcome. Turns out, once you relax, you're actually a cool guy."

"Because I was with you," he said, forcing himself to stand still as she smoothed his jacket, even though every instinct within him screamed that he should grab her, kiss her, and show her why their relationship would be so much more enjoyable if they let loose a little bit more, this time without those strict rules of hers. "I had fun."

"Me, too," she said softly. So softly he almost missed it. "Benjamin."

They fell silent, staring, almost as if they measured one another. The tension between them was impossible to ignore. Heart pounding, he reached out and ran his thumb over the curve of her chin, getting another hit of the drug that was Maggie Donovan. She shivered, gripping his jacket with a sigh. "You're so fucking unique and beautiful that I'm not even sure what to say to you half the damn time."

His words seemed to yank her from some sort of trance—the same trance he'd been stuck in. He hadn't meant to say that out loud...but even so, it was true. She was gorgeous, inside and out.

In his world, that was as rare as the Hope Diamond.

"You can say whatever you want, Benjamin." Stepping back, she tucked her hair behind her ear and gave him a shy smile. "I'll see you at the office Monday?"

"Yes. Of course." He shoved his trembling hands into his pockets and inclined his head. "I'll leave once I see you turn the light on, so I know you're safely inside."

She nodded and headed up the stairs, her hips swinging naturally. As soon as the light turned on, she pushed the curtain aside and waved at him. He nodded back, and slid inside his town car. After he closed the door, the driver pulled away.

No sooner had he cleared the curb, than his phone rang. When he saw who it was, he stiffened. He'd called his brother that morning, but hadn't gotten a hold of him. Apparently that was changing now. "Andrew. Thanks for calling me back."

"No problem," his brother's deep voice said through the line. "What's wrong?"

"Nothing. What makes you think something's wrong?"

Andrew paused. "Well, you called me."

"Yeah?"

"You never call unless something's wrong."

While true, it still hurt to hear. When had he become such a recluse that he forgot to pick up the damn phone and call his brother? "That's not true. I called you last week."

"For my birthday?" Andrew laughed. "Yeah, that doesn't count, Ben."

Benjamin winced, because he was right. "Sorry. Life's been busy."

"I hear you've been working constantly." He paused. "I also heard you have a new woman in the picture. One Mother doesn't approve of."

"Big shocker there."

Andrew laughed. "Who is she?"

"My lead researcher. We're…" He hesitated because he'd never lied to his brother before. "We're engaged, actually."

"Whoa! Another one bites the dust, huh?"

He rubbed his scalp. "Yeah. Something like that."

"That's great." Andrew exclaimed. Thing was, he actually sounded sincere. "When do I get to meet her?"

"She'll be at the mayor's dinner with me."

"Excellent." Andrew sighed. "Confirmed bachelor, Benjamin Gale the third, finally taken down by a woman. I can see the headlines now."

"Yeah." He rolled his eyes. "I'm dreading them already."

Andrew laughed. "I'm not."

Benjamin took a second and leaned his elbows on his knees. "Hey, did Mother tell you about the motion she wants to put forward?"

"No." Andrew's laughter died. "What's she up to now?"

"She wants to propose a motion of no confidence, on account of my nonstop philandering lifestyle." He paused.

"She wants you to take over as CEO."

"Shit." Andrew was silent a minute, then asked, "Is that why you're suddenly engaged? If so, don't do it. Don't give in to her insane demands."

"Nah, the engagement happened before this. We've been dating for a while now." Benjamin relaxed against the seat. It appeared that Andrew wasn't in on his mother's scheme, but that didn't mean he was going to come clean about the farce. "But you seriously weren't aware of it?"

"Of course not. I have no interest in taking your position."

At least he had one family member who wasn't trying to take him down.

Thank *God*.

Chapter Six

At exactly five o'clock Monday evening, Maggie closed her computer, slid it into her bag, took a deep breath, and stood. A few coworkers had already gathered their belongings, and they shot her some surreptitious glances the second she moved. She wasn't sure whether it was because she was leaving earlier than normal, or if it was because word had spread about her and Benjamin being engaged.

Either way...

They were freaking *staring*.

And they had been all day, too. At first it had been mildly amusing, but after the tenth person stopped by her desk to chat—correction, to *gape* at her ring—it had gotten old, really fast. Obviously, some sort of announcement was needed.

She might as well get it over with.

"Just do it, Maggie. Stand up, and announce you're dating Benjamin," she muttered under her breath. Fisting her hands at her sides, she cleared her throat loudly, ignoring her racing heart. "Yes, I've been secretly dating Mr. Gale, and yes, I have been since before I even started working here. And yes,

I'm engaged to him. He gave me a gorgeous ring." She led her hand up high, rotating it every which way. "Here it is. Now, can we all move on, and stop staring at me like I'm a freak?"

People ducked their heads, returning to whatever they'd been doing earlier. Maggie nodded once, smoothed her skirt, and headed for Benjamin's door.

That went surprisingly well.

Hopefully this next step would, too.

"You can do this. Everything will be fine," she whispered under her breath, staring at the Empire State Building as she went. She could just make out the red neon sign on top of the old New Yorker Hotel, too. "It's fine. This'll be fun. You're strong and steady, like that building. Benjamin won't make you cave. You won't kiss him or touch him. You're not going to lose."

If she said it enough times, maybe she'd actually believe it.

After a long, calming breath, she lifted her hand and knocked three times on his door. She heard a muffled "*come in*" through the wood, so she twisted the knob. She couldn't remember the last time she'd left the office before seven, and Benjamin rarely did either, but tonight…

They were going to do it together.

Be rebels.

It had taken most of the last two days to get everything lined up properly, but she was ready to show him what a *real* first date should be like. When she walked in, the frown he wore faded a tiny bit, and he studied her without lifting his head from his work. "Hey. How's it going out there?"

"Awkwardly. They're all staring." She waved a hand and tucked her hair behind her ear. He looked so handsome sitting behind his desk in his navy blue suit, with his perfect hair begging to be touched. "Like, constantly. I'm about to drag my desk in here so I can have a closed door, too."

He set his pen down and sighed. "Do I need to say something?"

"No, please. It's fine."

"Okay." He paused again, frowning. "Why are you in here, if you don't need my help?"

Her cheeks heated, because he seemed annoyed at her intrusion. "We're leaving."

"What?" He glanced at his watch and shook his head. "No way in hell. I've got at least two more hours of work here on my desk, and it's only five o'clock. Not to mention, you still haven't gotten me that report you owe me. I told you it would wait, but I didn't mean forever." His tone was dismissive, as if having dealt with her, he expected her to leave.

He was sadly mistaken.

The only way she was leaving was with him.

She crossed her arms and tapped her foot, fighting back the irritation rising within her at his tone. He wasn't making it hard to resist him with that attitude of his, so it really wasn't fair that she *still* wanted him.

Sighing, he glanced up again. "What now?"

"The same thing as before." She tapped her foot faster. "It's after hours. The 'boss' you has to go away, and my 'fiancé' needs to come out to play. We have a date."

That got his attention. He perked up and pushed his chair back. "In that case, come on over. Give me some sugar, darling."

She shook her head, despite the way her pulse leaped when he grinned at her roguishly and patted his lap. All she could think was: *yes please.*

After he'd stopped playing by the first-date playbook the other night, things between them had changed. It was like a switch had been turned off inside of him, and he'd become a different man. It had been hard to resist the more controlled version of him.

This version made it *impossible.*

Forcing herself to stay still and not climb onto his lap to purr louder than her cat, Lucifer, did when she groomed him, she crossed her arms. "Not *quite* what I had in mind."

"Pity." He gave her a darker, even more seductive look that made butterflies take off in her stomach and explode midflight. "What did you have in mind, then?"

"Me." She crept closer. "You." Leaning across his desk, she grabbed his tie and tugged him to his feet. The way he watched her, all hot and possessive, made her thighs quiver. "Leaving, together, in front of the whole office. The rest is a secret that you'll find out about when we get downstairs to our limo."

He cocked a brow. "You hired a limo?"

"Nah." She smiled and pulled him out from behind his desk by his tie. He came willingly, a barely leashed wildness emanating from every single muscle in his body. She swallowed hard, thinking that maybe, just maybe, she'd bitten off more than she could chew with Benjamin Gale. "I called your butler, and he told your driver to be waiting for us."

He gripped her hip, stepping into her personal space while not technically breaking any of the rules she'd laid out. "How did you get William's number?"

"I'm just that good." She yanked his tie one last time before letting go, trying her best to ignore the annoying voice inside of her that screamed for her to kiss him. "Now get your coat. We're leaving this office, hand in hand, so they see us being super cute."

He adjusted his abused tie, eyeing her. "You're being bossy. I kind of like it. It's hot."

She shot him a flirtatious smile, saying nothing. She was too busy trying to resist him to be witty.

He shrugged into his dark grey pea coat, never tearing his eyes off her, and a smile lit up his face. When he smiled, he chipped away at every defense she had in place against him. Lucky for her, *he* hadn't seemed to figure that out yet. "Are we going to get through this date without you running away again, or should I change into sneakers, just in case?"

"You never know." She walked up to him and held on to his jacket, staring up at him through her lashes. "We'll see how tonight goes."

"So this is a test?" Benjamin grinned and gripped her chin, tipping her face up to his. "If so, I intend to pass with flying colors. I don't like failing."

"I'm sure you don't." His mother had said almost the same exact thing, but she didn't point that out. "Which is why you're doomed for disappointment going up against me."

He came closer. "Have I told you how gorgeous you look today, Maggie? That red blouse really brings out the gray in your eyes."

Her heart fluttered, and she bit back a smile at his charming flirtation. His hold on her chin burned her skin and made her insides all jittery. She tried to hide that from him. He didn't need any more ammunition against her. "I don't have gray eyes."

"Sure you do." He tipped her face to his a little more. "But up close, when you smile, or try not to smile like you're doing right now, there are tiny little specks of blue, too. I plan on seeing those blue specks a lot in our time together. I discovered something about myself the other night. I like making you smile more than I like *anything*."

She took a deep breath, holding it in. She had no idea what to say to that. He'd literally rendered her speechless, making her doubt her ability to maintain her businesslike approach to this engagement, and they hadn't even left his office yet. "Benjamin…"

"Yes?" he asked, reaching out slowly and curling his hand securely around her nape. Then he lowered his head to hers. His lips were so close. Close enough that all it would take was a quick push from her heels, and she'd have what she wanted from him so badly, no matter how hard she tried to deny it. He held himself back, clearly waiting for her to give him a sign if his kiss was welcome or not. And that was the problem—it *was*. "What is it you need, darling?"

Oh, crap. He was pulling out nicknames now. She was so screwed. "Why do you keep calling me darling?"

"That's what you are to me." He lifted a shoulder and ran his thumb along her jaw. "And it seemed like a good fit. I was right. It feels good."

"Yeah…it does." And so did he, but she needed to keep her head on straight. She tugged free. He didn't let go right away. "But no one's in here, so there's no reason for us to kiss, right?"

"Right. Of course." His grip tightened for a second, and he pressed his mouth into a tight line, but then he let go. "Sorry."

She missed his touch immediately, but it was for the best. After she'd fought so hard to get it, she wasn't going to lose everything over a pretty face—although, to be fair, it wasn't just his face that had her swooning. It was everything—his smile, the way he slowly warmed up to her, and how he treated her differently than everyone else he interacted with. How he made her feel special with a simple smile or kind gesture. "Okay, so when we go out there, we'll go to my desk, and I'll grab my jacket. You take it from me, and help me put it on. I guess a soft kiss for their benefit will be permitted."

"Yes, ma'am," he said, his voice deeper than ever before.

She hesitated. "It's not that I don't want to kiss you, Benjamin. It's that I do."

He didn't say anything to that, just stared at her like she'd lost her mind.

But she knew herself better than he did, and she didn't

want to risk getting her heart broken over a guy who could never be hers for real. Not in a million years. But that didn't mean they couldn't become friends...hence this date she was taking him on.

From what she'd seen, and what he'd said, he was a loner. He never went out with the guys, or had a buddy drop by to say hi. To the best of her knowledge, he didn't have any friends at all. He needed a friend more than he needed yet another lover.

She had a feeling he didn't hurt in *that* area of his life.

He flexed his jaw, enfolded her hand in his, opened the office door, and inclined his head to the waiting office— which was still half filled with people packing up for the day. "Ladies first."

"Don't forget. Jacket, help, chaste kiss."

He nodded and repeated, "Yes, ma'am."

After taking a deep breath, she headed straight for her desk and grabbed her jacket as planned. The second she picked it up, he took it. "Please. Let me help you with that, darling," he said, deadpan.

People exchanged looks. They seemed less than impressed. If he kept up this emotionless acting, they could quit the charade right here and now. She shot him a frown as she slid her hands into the arms of her coat. "Thanks, Benji."

He choked and turned red. "*What the hell*? Never call me that ag—"

Grabbing his coat lapels before he blew everything she was trying to accomplish, she kissed him. His arms immediately closed around her. As with the last time, he snatched control of the kiss, commanding it *and* her to his will.

He seized her hips and yanked her closer to his body. A soft moan escaped her, because an impressively hard bulge pressed against her stomach, and she couldn't *help* it. She wanted him, despite all logic and reason telling her to keep her distance.

And if they had been alone, she might just have taken him.

Which was why they couldn't kiss in private. She *obviously* had no self-control when it came to Benjamin Gale. The first step to overcoming an obstacle was admitting to it… or however that cliché went. And her problem was Benjamin Gale.

She needed to get over it.

Tilting his head, he slanted his mouth across hers and teased her, running his tongue across her tightly sealed lips. She shouldn't let him—oh, screw it. She was opening her mouth and kissing him. Logic could kiss her butt. But when she gave him what he wanted, he pulled back, ending it without entering her mouth.

He didn't let go of her, though.

Instead, he smoothed her hair off her face and gave her a tender smile that, if she didn't know better, she'd swear was real. Pressing his cheek to her temple, he whispered, "You said to keep it chaste, right?"

"Huh?" She blinked, trying to get her thoughts back in order. Needing a break from his intense stare, she glanced around—and found every set of eyes on them. *Craaaaap.* How had she forgotten about their audience? At least he'd kept his knee firmly in check this time. She smoothed his jacket, even though it wasn't messed up at all, and stepped back. He let go of her. "Uh, right. That was perfect."

In more ways than one.

Stupid, sexy, irresistible man.

He buttoned her jacket for her and leaned down, pressing his mouth against her ear. "Just for the record, I can do that again later, when we don't have anyone watching us. I could have you naked, writhing, and screaming in my bed the second you gave me the green light. And you wouldn't regret a damn second of it."

Oh, I bet I would. She pressed her thighs together, but it did nothing to assuage the ache his words created inside her. "Benjamin, that's a horrible idea."

"It might be." He dropped one last kiss on her temple. "But I swear I'll make it worth your time...more than once." He skimmed his hand down her hip, barely touching her butt, since people were watching, and stepped back. After a quick glance at his crotch area, he tugged his jacket down to cover his erection. "And that's a fucking promise."

She bit her tongue to stop herself from moaning *again*, because she really, *really* wanted to collect on that. And she also wanted to lift that jacket up to get a better look.

Like...*really.*

Chapter Seven

Benjamin followed her down the sidewalk toward his waiting town car, adjusting his tight pants again. As she walked, her soft brown hair blew gently in the breeze, looking way too touchable to resist for long. And with her, he didn't want to resist at all. There was something about her that made him want to ignore years of self-restraint and controlled emotions. That made him want to be different. He wasn't sure if that was a bad thing or not, but he didn't give a damn.

He was going to roll with it. See where Maggie Donovan took him.

When she passed his town car, he stopped and cleared his throat. She glanced over her shoulder at him, her brow wrinkled. His heart rate increased just because she was so damn pretty, standing in the last afternoon sun on a busy New York street, wearing a black wool coat and a purple knit hat, staring at *him*. It did things to him.

Things he didn't fully understand.

The urge to pull her into his arms and kiss her, right there in front of all the people pushing past them, hit him like a fist to the gut. He didn't, though. Instead, he shoved his hands into his pockets and rocked back on his heels. After all, there was no one around to fool, so he wasn't supposed to kiss her. "You walking to our date, or what?"

"Oh, right." She shoved an errant piece of hair out of her face and shivered. Her cheeks were rosy red, just like the tip of her nose. "I zoned out for a second there."

He waved his driver off so he could open the door for her himself. "No worries."

She slid inside and peeked out at him. "I'm here now."

"Good." He followed her in and closed the door. Something smelled tantalizing and his stomach growled, but he couldn't quite place it. After he settled in, he teased her. "I'd be pretty damn bored if I was going on this date by myself."

Shaking her head, she glanced out the window and muttered, "But I'd be safer."

"Maggie." Even though she'd spoken, he had the feeling it hadn't been to him. "You're doing it again."

She startled, only further proving his point. "Doing what?"

"Talking to yourself."

"Yeah." She adjusted her skirt and shrugged. "I do that sometimes."

He smiled. He couldn't help it. "So you said."

"Oh." She blushed even more. "Right."

He turned her way. His thigh brushed hers, and she shivered before shifting closer to her side of the car. For the first time in he didn't know how long, he was *excited*. This date was going to tell him more about Maggie. What she liked. How she thought. What kind of woman she was. And he couldn't fucking wait to find out so he could blow her mind when it was his turn to pick the date again.

"Where are we going?"

"You'll see." The car pulled away from the curb, and she smiled, seeming to shake off some of her nerves. "First? Close your eyes."

"Are you going to strip naked for me? If so, I'm not closing my damn eyes."

She rolled hers. "Not a chance."

Sighing dramatically, he leaned back against the seat and did as she requested. His heart sped up, because even doing something as juvenile as closing his eyes so she could surprise him was exciting. Fresh. *Fun*. He couldn't remember the last time he'd had fun, before she'd crashed into his life. "Fine. My eyes are closed."

She waved her hand in front of his face. He felt it. When he didn't react, she pulled something out that crinkled. After setting it on his lap, she dusted off her hands. "Okay. Open them."

He did, and glanced down at his lap. A Wendy's bag sat in his lap, hot and greasy and artery clogging—but so fucking good. "Is that…?"

"A spicy chicken sandwich and cheese fries?" She grinned, looking way too damn proud of herself. "You bet your last cow it is."

His last *cow*? The things that came out of her mouth…

His stomach groaned in anticipation, and he stared at the bag. This was his favorite bad meal, his vice. He'd lived off this shit in college, but he hadn't had it in…God, at least six years. "How did you find out?"

"Oh, I'm just that good," she said again. Leaning back, she grinned and pulled out her own bag. "Eat up. I won't judge you…much."

And the thing was, it was true. She wouldn't judge him for…well, anything. And that was so refreshing and amazing that he wasn't sure what to do with it. Or her. He opened the bag, his mouth watering. "I'm going to have to do double time at the gym tonight after this, but it's worth it."

"Is that when you work out?" she asked, dropping a fry into her mouth. He couldn't look away from her lips. "At night?"

"Yeah." Clearing his throat, he pulled his own meal out. "I do it before bed."

She swallowed. "Where do you go?"

"My place." He opened the lid of his cheese fries. "I have a gym there."

She rolled her eyes. "Of course you do. I should've guessed."

They fell into companionable silence as they ate. By the time they finished, he felt a hundred pounds heavier, but more satisfied than a college kid after a night in a strip club. If someone had told him he'd eat Wendy's on a date with his fiancée, he'd have laughed till he fell over.

Yet, here he was.

"Thanks for the dinner," he said, wiping his hands off with a napkin.

She did the same, grinning. "You're welcome."

So. First tip? She liked Wendy's. Not expensive restaurants. "Now that we've stuffed ourselves..." Looking outside, he tried to figure out where they were. They were approaching Penn Station, heading down Eighth Avenue. "What's next?"

"This." She handed him a beer. His mother had always said it was a poor man's drink, and he was never to be seen with one in his hand. He didn't agree, but he also refused to give her yet another thing to bitch about. "Drink up."

He tightened his hold, remembering how much he'd enjoyed beer, once upon a time. "Where did you find out about *this*?"

"That you drink the best wines and whiskeys in public, but truly prefer a twenty-bucks-a-case bottle of beer?" She lifted hers to her lips. "Oh, I have my ways, Benjamin."

He studied her, lifting his own beer to his mouth to take a swig. It meshed well with the Wendy's he'd just eaten. He'd asked her to show him what she liked in a date, and instead of taking him to some pottery exhibit or boring art exhibit—she was giving him everything *he* liked instead. It didn't make any sense. Why would she do that?

Why would she care?

Lost in thought, he swished the beer in his mouth before swallowing. "Let me guess." He swirled the amber liquid in the bottle. "Our destination is a place that most people wouldn't suspect I like to go to, but you somehow discovered it."

Her lips twitched, and he saw those blue flecks in her eyes that he'd come to crave more than anything else. "Fine. I'll tell you. We're going to the Rangers game."

Jesus. She'd done her homework, all right. If he wasn't aware it was what she did for a living, it might've creeped him out. He understood now why she'd been upset at his botched attempt at a date Saturday night. It was painfully clear that she'd put a shitload of thought into this outing, into the things he'd like, and all he'd done was take her on his generic first date—and he'd assumed she'd be just as lost in his charm as other woman always had been. Maggie was a special kind of woman.

The kind who cared more about *his* fun than *hers*.

He swallowed hard, shame churning in his gut. "Let me guess. You found out because you're just that good?"

"Nah. That one was easy to figure out all on my own," she said, laughing. "You have a puck on the corner of your desk."

And *that* made him feel even worse. She was so much better at this than he was. He was used to skating through life without a care, getting what he wanted from people with a snap of his fingers, and he'd dared to treat her like the rest of the people in his life.

He wouldn't make that mistake again.

A few hours later, in the last seconds of the game, Benjamin shot to his feet, a beer clasped precariously in his left hand. The opposing team had slammed a Ranger into the wall, and a fight broke out. "Get the piece of shit!" he shouted, laughing when the Ranger knocked the other guy to his ass. "Fuck yeah!" As soon as the words left his lips, he looked at Maggie. "Sorry. So sorry."

She laughed. When she was chilly and rosy, she had freckles that danced across her nose and cheeks. "You can shout curses in front of me. I won't faint."

People started clearing out of the arena, but he didn't move. Neither did she. Truth be told, he didn't want the night to end. It had been...*fun*. So much fucking fun it was almost like a dream. Like he'd fallen asleep at his desk and would soon wake up with his head resting on a stack of reports, instead of having Maggie at his side.

If that was the case, he didn't want to wake up. He wanted to stay where he was.

He enjoyed hanging out with Maggie, and if they got up, it would be over. She'd go home, and he'd go home, and he'd be alone in his apartment, like always.

Funny. That didn't sound as appealing as it had a week ago.

"But still." He sat back down, his knee brushing against hers. He clenched his jaw. All night long, those accidental touches had been killing him, and she suffered, too. He saw the tension in her growing with each soft touch. He felt it, too. "It's a respect thing. Gentlemen shouldn't curse in front of ladies."

She snorted. "Lucky for you I'm not a lady. I'm just me."

"Ah, but I disagree." He turned Maggie's way, and those gray eyes of hers were glowing with so much *life*. And, damn it, he wanted to feel that way, too. To remember what it felt like when he'd been...well, himself. "You're more of a lady, and more deserving of respect, than anyone else I've ever met. You're amazing Maggie, and don't let anyone else tell you otherwise."

She swallowed hard and shifted closer to him. "Thank you."

"You're welcome." He glanced away, before he did the unthinkable and touched her cheek, or gave up resisting, broke the rules, and kissed her. The worst part was he could see the matching desire burning in her eyes, but she refused to give in. "And I'm sorry for my outburst."

All his life, he'd been taught to hide his emotions. To never show happiness, fear, or even excitement. For a while, he'd balked against those constraints. He'd been *alive*. But then his father had died, and all that had changed. Around Maggie, the balance shifted again. Tiny pieces of the real him came out to play.

And it was good to get a portion of himself back.

"It makes me happy, seeing you so..." She set a soft hand on his arm. "Free."

He couldn't see it, since he'd refocused on the ice, but he could feel it deep down to his soul. It was as if when she touched him, she somehow made him brighter—which was ridiculous. "I'm not free."

"And you never will be, with your mother on your back."

He lifted a shoulder, watching the Zamboni smooth the ice. "It's fine. She's just got a set of goals in mind for me, and when I don't follow through with her plans, she gets upset."

That, and she hates me—for good reason. But he wouldn't

say that out loud. It would only sound like a pity party, and he didn't do those.

"I get that," she said softly. She sipped her beer, also watching the machine as it smoothed away the blemishes in the ice. Too bad they didn't make those for your life. Benjamin could think of a few incidents he'd like to smooth over, too. Maggie went on. "My ex was like that. Overbearing. Controlling. Irrational."

He glared down at his beer. "I hope you kicked him to the curb quick."

"Not quick enough." She side-eyed him. "Not before I needed a court order against him to make him to leave me alone."

He growled deep in his throat, not even meaning to. The fact that she'd been scared enough—hurt enough—to need an injunction infuriated him. "What's his name? I'll kill him."

"No need." She smiled, but it was a sad one. "He did that himself, after writing me a note that told me it was all my fault."

He swallowed. That kind of history explained so much about her reluctance to let him in. To trust him. Hell, he didn't blame her. Not after what she'd been through. And the worst part was, Maggie was the kindest person he'd ever met. She didn't deserve that. "It wasn't your fault," he said.

"Maybe it was, maybe it wasn't." She lifted the beer to her lips. "Either way, it only proves how bad I am at relationships. It's why I stopped trying. He wasn't the first guy to show me that love isn't worth the fight, but I swore he'd be the last."

Which was why she refused to let him kiss her. She was scared they'd come to a messy end. And even with all of that, she had gone through a hell of a lot of effort to give him the best date he'd ever had. She'd shown him kindness he could never, and *had* never, shown another person. It was humbling, and embarrassing, and it made him like her even more.

He'd needed her to reminded him what it was like to open yourself up and let another person in. And, against all reason, he wanted that person to be *her*. He wanted all of her. Even if he didn't deserve her.

"Christ." He shook his head and glared down at his beer. "I'm sorry."

She froze, her beer still at her lips. Lowering it, she swiped her hand across her mouth. "What for?"

"For not putting in even a fraction of the effort that you've obviously put into this date." He reached out and caught her hand, and for once she didn't pull away. "I'll do better next time. I swear it."

She swallowed hard. "It's fine. I mean, it's not like we're *actually* dating."

He'd become so good at hiding his desires and emotions that he'd forgotten how to voice them out loud. But with Maggie, he wanted to, and he wanted to stop pretending that she was just a way for him to keep his position. "So you keep saying."

She sipped her beer, not meeting his eyes. "Well, that's because it's true."

He had the distinct impression she said that out loud for her benefit instead of his. He also suspected that she didn't believe it any more than he did, because it felt fucking real. Right here, right now, it did. "It doesn't matter anymore if this is real, or if it isn't. I think you're fooling yourself, and me. Or maybe I am."

Her breath whooshed out. "I'm not sure what you're saying."

"That's because I'm not making any sense," he said, frustration clear in his tone. He rested a hand on her thigh. It trembled under his touch. "You obviously put a hell of a lot of thought into this date, which either means you wanted to prove a point about how much I screwed up Saturday night—"

"What?" She shook her head. "No. Not at all."

He continued as if she hadn't spoken. "Or you care about what I think and feel, and wanted to make me happy."

She swallowed hard. "Yeah. And so what if I do?"

"It's been a hell of a long time since anyone gave a damn what I wanted. This thing we have between us? It's no longer just for show. Not on my end." He gritted his teeth, trying to think of the best way to articulate his thoughts without sounding like an idiot. "I want you."

"Benjamin…"

"Tell me you don't want me, and I'll never mention this again." He held on to her chin with his thumb and forefinger, keeping his touch gentle enough for her to turn away if she wanted. She didn't. "Tell me you don't want me to fuck you. Tell me I'm wrong."

She closed her mouth, opened it, and said, "You're not wrong. I do. But—"

"Shh." He pressed a finger to her mouth. "You don't want to want me, because you think it's a horrible idea, and that I'm going to hurt you like all the guys before me."

"Right," she whispered, her eyes drifting shut. "And you're my boss, so when that happens, it'll be even worse. That's why it's a terrible idea."

When he hurt her. Not *if.*

She was so certain that's how they would end, and he wasn't sure how he felt about that—besides the fact that he didn't like it. "All great ideas start with bad ones. No one gets it right all the time."

She swallowed. "But this is all happening so fast, and—"

"It's not, though." He removed his finger from her soft, kissable lips. Lips he couldn't have. "I've wanted you ever since the first day you started working for me. You walked into my office with your hair down. You wore that black skirt, and a blue blouse, with a pair of black heels. Do you remember what you said to me?"

A small sound escaped her, and she stared at him as if she couldn't believe he remembered what she wore that day. "I think I told you my name, and informed you that I intended to be the best researcher you'd ever met."

"I think you've become that." He smiled. "That's how you made this happen tonight. You researched, right?"

"Seriously. I was just trying to give you a good night," she said quickly. "It was nothing."

"If you want it to be nothing," he said slowly, locking gazes with her. "It can be nothing. Or, it can be something."

"What do you mean?"

"I mean if you don't want more, I'll make sure you never find out how much I want to kiss you again, or how it's all I think about. I'll stop telling you that what you did for me tonight means something, something *real*, and I'll act like I don't give a shit." He lifted a shoulder. "I'm good at that. I've had a lot of practice at hiding what I think and feel."

"I'd never want that." She shook her head. "Don't hide your feelings from me."

He smiled slightly. "Fine. You want honesty?"

"Uh…" She hesitated, but nodded. "Sure. Go for it."

"In just these few short days, you've made me feel things I wasn't sure I could anymore, and I think you could do a hell of a lot more, if we both let you."

"Benjamin—"

"I know. I know." He let go of her. "You're not interested. But I had to say it. For the first time in years, I want to lay it all out there, in the open for all to see, because you deserve nothing less."

"Why do you feel like you have to hide your emotions at all?" she asked.

He sucked in a breath, watching her. He wasn't sure if he was ready for this conversation.

She must have seen the panic in his eyes. "Never mind. It's—"

"No." He reached out and rested a hand on hers. "My father had a heart attack. While they rushed him to the hospital, I was out drinking and getting laid. I didn't even make it home before he died, and ever since, I've been trying to make up for that. I never will, but it doesn't keep me from trying."

She watched him closely, as if everything suddenly made sense to her. As if she understood him better now, and he wasn't sure how he felt about that. And that uncertainty in the face of opening up to someone was what a real date was supposed to be like. "That wasn't your fault. You had no way of knowing he would die that night."

She was wrong. It *was* his fault. "It doesn't matter. That's in the past. I want to talk about now." He cupped her cheek and gave her a small smile. "And right now? I want you. I want you so damn bad it hurts. And not just because I want to fuck you. I want *all* of you, Maggie."

"I…" Her lids drifted shut, and she let out a small, almost broken sound. "I'm not sure what to say."

Something stabbed him in the chest, sending a piercing phantom pain throughout his body. He'd known she didn't want him, but it still hurt. "Do you want me to take it back? To pretend this conversation never happened?"

"I—*no*." She hesitated, but shook her head. "I don't want that at all."

A strong surge of gratification rushed through him. He'd given her an out, and she hadn't taken it. "How about this? We treat this whole going out and spending time together like a real thing between us—not romantic, necessarily, but friends. I like you, Maggie, and I want to be your friend."

Swallowing hard, she nodded once. "I'd like that, Benjamin."

"Then let's be real with one another and see where things go. If they turn romantic, we'll deal with that when it comes." He shrugged. "But if we stay just friends for the rest of our lives, and *only* friends, I'm fine with that, too. But I'm not going to lie. I'm hoping for more. And I think you are, too."

And he would stop at *nothing* to make sure they both got what they wanted.

She bit the corner of her lower lip. "This thing wouldn't work. You're from a different world than I am. We might be able to make it work for the short-term, fake engagement, but real feelings? It would never hold. Statistically speaking, we're—"

"Do you always read the end of the book before the beginning?"

She lowered her head and peeled her label off her beer. "Well, actually, yeah. I do. Every time."

"Why do you do that?" he asked.

She shrugged, still staring down at her bottle. "So I know what to expect. I like advance warning, so I don't get attached to anyone or anything that doesn't make it to the end."

"That might work in fiction, but in real life?" He caught her hand, stopping her from peeling the label off any more than she already had. "You can't skip ahead to the end, especially not with us. There's no way in hell to know how it'll end."

"But—" Her fingers curled into a fist inside his. "Yeah, okay. You're right."

"We'll take it slow. *Real* slow. Spend time together. Start at the beginning of our story, and we'll figure out the end when we get there." He gave her a small smile. "So, what do you say? Do you want to read our story with me?"

She laughed. "Oh my God. I can't believe I'm saying this...but yes. *Slowly*. As friends."

"Excellent." He grinned, resisting the urge to pick her

up and kiss her. He'd just gotten her agreement to give him a chance to—hell, he wasn't sure what the hell he was doing when it came to Maggie. But he'd figure it out as he went, like he'd said. Lifting her hand to his mouth, he kissed her knuckles. "I can't wait to get to the sex scenes, though. I assure you, they'll be worth a second read."

She laughed, throwing her head back. It was the prettiest sound he'd ever heard, hands down. "You're incorrigible, Benji."

He scowled. "About that name—"

"I tried it on for size because it felt right." She shot him a cocky grin and finished off her beer. The crowds around them had thinned out. "I was right. It stays."

"Fine, *darling*." He stood up and helped her to her feet, holding on to both of her hands. His blood rushed hotter when she didn't immediately move away. "If it stays, so does this."

Lowering his head, he gave her plenty of time to back off, or turn away. She didn't. She actually fisted his jacket and tugged him closer, so he melded his mouth to hers. He kept the kiss sweet and short, not wanting to push her too hard or too fast. When he pulled back, his entire body protesting the motion, he rested his forehead on hers.

Her breasts touched his chest, and she clung to him. It took every ounce of his self-control not to press closer to her. To not take more than a damn kiss.

Being with her, holding her in his arms, made everything thing seem brighter. Happier. Shinier. He had no fucking idea what any of that meant, but there was no denying it anymore. He'd never wanted to have someone so badly before, and that definitely meant something, so he'd keep his hands to himself. Keep his eye on the goal. Be patient. Caring. Understanding.

And in the end…he'd *win*.

Chapter Eight

Four days.

That was how long she and Benjamin had been hanging out, after agreeing at the hockey game to become friends for real, *after* becoming fake engaged. Backward, yes, but whatever. It was working…as long as she ignored the fact that she wanted him so much it physically hurt. Which was stupid.

She'd always been good at making logical decisions. She never made a choice without thinking through all the details and possibilities. Some might even say she overanalyzed everything—and they'd be right. She totally did.

Except when it came to Benjamin Gale.

When it came to him, she wasn't *rational* at all.

They'd spent the last few days getting to know one another. Turned out, they had a lot more in common than being workaholics. They both liked hockey and basketball, and cats more than dogs. They preferred dark chocolate, and when he laughed, it made her think that maybe she was crazy for holding herself away from him.

She liked him. A lot.

Which was why she was *so* screwed.

They hadn't kissed or done anything that wasn't strictly on a "just friends" level since the night of the hockey game. He'd been one hundred percent proper at all times. If she was honest with herself, she missed the way he used to be. She'd give anything to have him look at her as if he wanted nothing more than to see what she wore underneath her skirts and blouses. She couldn't think about anything else but finding out what lay beneath those suits.

The office quieted, so she glanced up.

If they were quiet, that meant...

"Hey," Benjamin said, his deep voice sending a shiver down her spine like always. He wore a navy blue suit, a green shirt, and a striped gray tie. He looked as impeccably handsome as ever, and her stomach tightened at his proximity. Resting his big, calloused hands on her desk, he leaned close, lowering his voice so only she could hear him. "Shouldn't you be gone by now, getting ready for tonight?"

She swallowed and set down her pen. Tonight was her debut in his world, at the mayor's freaking ball. No pressure or anything. It wasn't as if she was meeting anyone important, or being seen by anyone important. Just, ya know...

The *Mayor of New York freaking City.*

"I think this is a horrible idea," she said for what had to be the billionth time.

He sighed. "So you keep saying. And as *I* keep saying, you'll do fine. Did you use my card to get your outfit?"

"Yes. But—"

He rubbed his jaw. "It's red, right?"

"Yes."

A quick nod of his head. "I'll wear my red bowtie."

"How can you be so *calm* about this?" She stood and tossed her glasses on the desk. "I'll make a fool out of myself, and you, and you'll regret ever asking—"

He held a hand up, his jaw flexing. "You can stop that sentence right now, because I already told you I don't regret a damn thing. Go home. Start getting ready."

"You're being stubborn."

"And you're procrastinating by trying to pick a fight." He straightened her computer, and folded her reading glasses on top of it. He hated when things were out of order—she'd learned that about him, too. "It won't work, because you're too adorable to annoy me."

She smiled for the first time that day. She couldn't help it. "Benji."

"Not even that annoying nickname will work tonight." Lowering his head, he straightened her pens in color-coded order.

Licking her lips, she watched as his long fingers moved over her stuff. Her breath quickened, and her pulse sped up. "Can't blame a girl for trying."

He snorted. "The hell I can't."

Not answering, she stared at those fingers with a thirst that wouldn't be quenched, and more than anything, she wanted them on *her*—not her pens. The more time she spent with him, the stronger the thirst became.

"Now go—" When he lifted his head again, he froze. "Stop looking at me like that."

She tilted her head. "Like what?"

He leaned in even closer, and her heart picked up even more speed. His eyes sparked, igniting a primal urge inside of her, and he whispered for her ears only, "Like you want to get me naked, and once and for all stop this 'just friends' bullshit we're both suffering through."

She grasped the edge of her desk so hard it hurt. "I'm not sure what you're talking about."

"Yeah, you are. I—" He glanced over his shoulder and stiffened, because everyone was watching them. Big shocker there. "Just go home and get ready. I'll pick you up in two hours, and you'll look gorgeous."

"But—"

He pointed to the door. "*Go.*"

"Fine." Frowning, she picked up her jacket and purse, her legs trembling. "But don't say I didn't warn you."

He didn't reply, just scowled at her like the beast that people assumed he was. She huffed one last time and left, his stare burning into her back. As soon as she was in the elevator, she pulled out her phone. *On my way home.*

Becca texted back quickly. *I just left the office, too, and picked up some new makeup with that card. Meet you there.*

How was work?

Again, her phone buzzed with Becca's response. *Boring. Some asshole wasn't sure what he wanted for his campaign, and I spent hours discussing the merits of billboard advertising versus online.*

Maggie winced. *Sounds fun.*

Oh yeah. So much. The little bubble with three dots appeared. *I can't wait to go out with Patrick later. I need a distraction.*

Still seeing him?

For now. I'm not bored yet. Still avoiding admitting you want your billionaire?

The elevator doors opened. *Yep. Okay, I have to go. See you there.*

By the time she actually got to their apartment twenty minutes later, Becca waited for her outside their door. She had a brown bag in one hand, and a makeup kit in the other. Her long red hair blew in the breeze. When she saw Maggie, she straightened and held up the hand with the brown bag. "I brought vodka to go with the makeup."

"Good. I need it. Why are you outside? You live here, too."

"I was enjoying the sun. It's been a while since we had a nice day, and after being in the office all day…" Becca shrugged. "It felt good."

She looked up at the blue sky. The sun shone through the skyscrapers and clouds, right onto them. "It is really nice out."

"Yeah." Her best friend pushed off the wall and unlocked the door. "And you were too busy panicking to notice. Why are you so nervous, anyway? It's just a stupid party."

"It's not *just* a party. It's the first test—we have to sell this whole thing tonight."

Becca shrugged. "It'll be fine. It's not like they'll be giving you a lie detector to see if your relationship is legit. All you have to do is drink free booze, hold his hand, and act like you're in love with a guy you haven't stopped blabbering on about all week long. It shouldn't be too much of a stretch."

"No, it's not, and that's exactly why I don't want to go."

Becca blinked. "I'm sorry, what?"

"Benjamin and I are only friends, and I really need it to stay that way, no matter what my stupid ovaries want. But we haven't even kissed in four days—which is why I need the drink," she said, snatching the bottle from her friend's hand and heading into the kitchen. "Because, God, I want him, Becca. I want him *bad*."

"No kidding," Becca said drily.

"I'm an idiot."

"Yeah." She pushed her red hair out of her face. "Always have been, when it comes to men."

Maggie frowned and pulled out two shot glasses. "Gee, thanks."

"You overanalyze everything, and push every interested man out of the picture before they even have a chance to mess up." Becca hopped up on the counter, swinging her legs. "It's your MO."

"That's because none of them ever make sense," Maggie argued, pouring two shots. "Why waste my time when they never add up on paper?"

Her best friend shrugged. "And they never will. Which

is why you do it, if you ask me. It gives you an excuse to get rid of them before they get too close and hurt you, like those other jerks did when you first moved here."

That hit uncomfortably close to home. "That's not true. It's not my fault the men I've dated aren't committed enough to prove me wrong."

"You've been trying to keep this CEO of yours at a distance, haven't you?"

"Yeah." She tossed back the shot. "And?"

"And he hasn't given up yet." Becca joined her, downing the vodka. "Maybe he's the guy you've been waiting for. The one who will fight for you."

But what if he did? What if she let him win? They would sleep together, have a little fun, and when he realized the two of them didn't make sense together—as he inevitably would—he would move on. She'd be left working for a man who no longer acted as if she existed, *and* she'd have a front row seat to all the society girls he paraded in front of her.

Maggie groaned. "You're not helping matters. I'm supposed to listen to my head, not you, not my ovaries, and certainly *not* my heart."

"If you ask me, you've done enough listening to your head. Maybe it's time to try something new," she argued, holding her hands up when Maggie scowled at her. "You could do worse than a rich CEO. That's all I'm saying."

"He doesn't show any emotion. Like, ever." She set the shot glass down. She refilled the glass and picked it up, glaring down at the ring it left on her counter. "I can never even begin to guess what he's thinking. It's infuriating."

"So ask him."

She snorted. "And when we break up—"

"You're not even *together* yet." Becca sighed and jumped off the counter. "You need to stop guessing how it's going to end, and enjoy the ride."

"Ugh. You sound like him."

"Then he's a smart man," she said, picking up the new makeup she'd stopped at the store to get. She steered Maggie toward the bedroom, her hands on her shoulders as she propelled her forward. "Listen to us."

"Like you listened to me when I told you Patrick was a bad idea?"

The other woman shrugged, not meeting Maggie's eyes. "Yeah, he's a bad idea. That's why I picked him."

"But—"

"Uh uh." She pointed at Maggie. "This is my lecture, not yours. You have a rich hottie who wants to become your friend *before* getting in your pants, which is practically unheard of in the dating world nowadays, and you're too busy worrying what other people will think of you to *enjoy* it."

Well, when she said it like that...screw them. Screw everything. Maggie was gonna have some fun with Benjamin, and stop stressing so much.

Maybe it was the booze, or the pep talk, but Becca was right. She had spent her whole life not caring what people thought of her. Why should that change now? What was it about Benjamin, and his witch of a mother, that brought out the worst in her? Whatever it was, she was over it.

And she was done pushing Benjamin away, too.

Becca was right. It was time to take a leap of faith, for once in her life, and hope for the best. Maybe it was time to stop thinking so much, and start doing.

Turning, she hugged her best friend close. "I love you. What would I do without you here to tell me off?"

"I'm not sure." Becca kissed the side of her head. "But lucky for you, you'll never have to find out. You ready to kick some rich ass now?"

"Yep." Grinning, she snapped her fingers. "Let's do this. Make me a princess."

Chapter Nine

Benjamin frowned at Maggie's brownstone, his heart pounding harder than a racehorse's hooves in the home stretch at the Kentucky Derby. He hadn't been this nervous since... *ever.* He'd never been the anxious type, not even when he was younger. If shit needed to get done, he did it. If it was going to be a rough night, he grinned and bullshitted his way through it.

His mother had made it perfectly clear he was expected to bring someone proper to the party—and drop his "fiancée" like a hot potato—or he'd pay the price. He'd kindly told her to go to hell, and that he would bring Maggie to the party, and she would deal with it. But now that the moment was here, his palms were sweating, his heart was racing, and he felt as if he'd just finished running ten miles at the gym.

The second he brought Maggie into his world, she'd be subjected to all the petty snarkiness that was served in heaping portions at these events, alongside the champagne and caviar...which he probably should have thought about earlier, but he'd been too caught up in the plan.

Too caught up in *her*. In how she made him *feel*.

She had a hold on him that he couldn't escape or deny, and he'd stopped trying a while ago. He wasn't going to confess his undying love for her, or anything so dramatic as that. That was still a foreign emotion he wasn't sure existed. But she was funny, kind, smart, and beautiful in every way. And the more time he spent with her, the more he became susceptible to those qualities. It was like she was slowly weaving a spell over him, dragging him further and further underwater until he ran out of breath and stopped fighting.

But she wanted to be friends, and he'd been cooling his heels for a week. He was starting to think he might need to be rescued via copter before he died in the damn friend zone she'd cursed him to. But he'd be *fine*. They would both be *fine*. If he said that enough times, he might actually believe it.

Pigs might fly, too. The world was full of surprises.

His driver opened the door, and Benjamin slid out of the seat, holding the flowers he'd gotten her close to his chest. Tugging at his red bowtie, he walked up her stairs, smoothed his tux, and knocked. Almost immediately, the door opened. He smiled, but it faded when he noticed it was a redhead who answered, not his Maggie.

After glancing at the number of the brownstone to make sure he was at the right building and knocking on the right door, since they were all the same on this block, he turned back to the woman in the door. "Hello. You must be Maggie's roommate. I'm—?"

"Damn." The redhead looked him up and down. "She didn't say you were *this* hot."

"Uh…" Yeah. He had nothing to say to that. He held his hand out politely. "I'm Benjamin Gale the third. And you are…?"

"The third, huh? Wow. So official sounding," the woman said, laughing lightly and shaking his hand before letting go.

She picked up her purse and smiled. "I'm Becca Marigold, the first, and I was just leaving for my own date. Maggie's in her room finishing up, so she'll be out in a minute."

He bowed and moved out of her way, still holding the flowers to his chest. "It was lovely meeting you, Ms. Marigold."

"Likewise," she said drily. "Good call on the flowers. She hates roses."

He glanced down at them. Damn, he'd really screwed up on that first date. Wrong restaurant. Wrong flowers. Wrong everything. It was a miracle she'd agreed to give him a second chance, and it only went to show how incredible she was, and that he didn't deserve her. "Thanks."

After shooting him one last look, the woman let the door close behind her.

He was alone in Maggie's living room. Glancing around, he swallowed hard. The whole place, while clean, was best described as organized chaos. Pillows lay askew on the couch, and she had books and magazines strewn all over the place in no semblance of order. There were empty mugs sitting on the coffee table, and a few blankets tossed here and there.

His fingers twitched. "Maggie? I'm here."

"I'll be out in a second. Make yourself comfortable," she called out.

He eyed the sofa and took a deep breath. When the door opened and she came out, he was sitting on the couch with the flowers resting on his thighs. The second he saw her, all thought fled. She walked into the room in a red dress that clung to her every curve. It had beaded lace overlaying the material underneath, and her long brown hair fell around her bare shoulders in soft, gentle waves.

Her red lips matched her dress, and she clutched a small black purse in front of her. Her white knuckles betrayed her nerves, and he wanted to kiss her so much it *hurt* him not to do so. Not trusting himself to speak, he examined her and tried to find logical words to say. He failed horribly.

She was too beautiful for mere words.

Shifting on her feet, she nibbled on her lip. "Are you going to say something? Anything? Will I pass for your impoverished fiancée?"

"Yes—" His voice croaked, so he cleared his throat and stood awkwardly, still not able to look away. He'd never seen anyone more stunning than her, and never would. Of that he was sure. "Yes. You…you look exquisite."

"Thank you." She relaxed slightly and her knuckles went a little less white on her clutch. "Are those for me?"

"Is what for you?"

Her lips twitched. "The flowers in your hands."

"Oh." Surprised, he glanced down. They'd slipped his mind the second she stepped into the room. What the hell did flowers matter when Maggie was there, smiling at him and looking as if she came straight out of a dream? "Yes, sorry."

"It's okay," she said, her smile widening. Those freckles of hers danced, making her all the more delectable. She took the bouquet from him and lifted them to her nose. Inhaling deeply, hugged them to her chest. "Snowbells. Good guess—I love these."

"I didn't guess." He'd never been so jealous of flowers in his life. "You told me you liked them last week."

"Oh." She blinked. "You remembered?"

"Well, yeah." He scratched the back of his head and shrugged. "I told you I'd try to do bett—*oof.*"

Before he could finish, she'd tossed the flowers onto the couch and threw herself at him. He stumbled back a step before catching himself and closing his arms around her. He had no clue what he did to get such a reward, but he rested his cheek on her head and enjoyed it anyway. When she hugged him close, something deep within him warmed.

Something he didn't recognize…or *want* to recognize.

And when she pulled back, ending the hug way too quickly, he was almost relieved because those unfamiliar emotions freaked him out. He tightened his hold on her hips, torn between wanting to pull her back into his arms or to push her away. That had been the first time she'd touched him intimately—because, hell yes, a hug like that was intimate in his book—of her own accord, and not part of their deception.

"What was that for?"

She smiled up at him. "The flowers."

Ah. The flowers. Not just the act of flowers, since he'd done that before and she couldn't have cared less, but the *type* he'd gotten. Well, hell, if he got a hug every time he did something thoughtful for her, he'd do it all the damn time.

He was all about rewards. Especially when it came to Maggie.

A stray piece of hair fell across her face, so he pushed it away from her cheek gently, staring into her eyes as he did so. It might be cliché, but damned if he couldn't get lost in those swirling blue-grey depths for hours if she let him. "You're welcome."

Moving out of his arms, she picked the flowers up and walked across the room. Halfway there, she stopped and glanced back at the couch with a frown. "Did you…did you straighten up in here? The pillows…and the coffee mugs… and where are my shoes?"

Shit.

She'd noticed.

"Well…I…" He eyed the neatened couch nervously, and the shoes he'd set by the door. He hadn't meant to do it, it had just sort of happened. "Uh…you did say to make myself at home."

She laughed, the musical sound washing over him. "I did, didn't I? It's cool. I don't care if you need to make my couch pretty to sit on it, Benji."

It's not that he *needed* to. It's that for his whole life, he'd had his mother telling him that he had to put on his best face, and never let anyone see him in anything but perfect order. That had stuck with him and made him the man he was today. One that liked order instead of chaos. But he didn't say any of that.

Why would he?

So he just tugged on his bowtie and checked the time. "Once you're ready, we need to go."

"Okay, just give me a second," she called out from the kitchen. "I'll be right out."

He grabbed her jacket off the chair where she'd thrown it, straightened the pillow, and waited by the door. When she came out, the oxygen disappeared from the room all over again. Something of what he felt must have shown on his face, because she paused mid-step. "What? What is it?"

"Nothing. It's just… You look absolutely gorgeous." He swallowed, but it was harder than it should have been. "You'll be the prettiest woman there, inside and out."

"Thanks. But I'm seriously unqualified to be going to this event."

"Bullshit. You don't ever have to be nervous walking into a room full of stuck-up snobs, because you're better than all of them combined." He crossed the room and stopped in front of her, toe-to-toe. "You're too good for me. So thank you for doing this."

She licked her red lips, her cheeks almost matching her lipstick. "I'm not too good for you, Benji."

He didn't meet her eyes. "Yes. You are." He skimmed his knuckles over the soft skin of her arm, watching with fascination as goose bumps rose where he touched. An answering desire crashed through him. "But the fact that you don't realize that? It's what makes you so damn special."

She didn't say anything. Just stared at him.

The pull between the two of them was overwhelming, and it took every single damn ounce of his self-control not to kiss her. If he broke down and did it, he wouldn't be able to stop. And he'd promised to take things slow, as friends—like the dumb-ass he was.

When he didn't lean in and close the distance between them, he swore he saw a flash of disappointment run across her expression. Though maybe that was wishful thinking on his part because, damn it, he wished she wanted him as much as he wanted her.

"We should go," she said softly. Turning her back to him, she peeked over her shoulder. He didn't move, just clutched her jacket tightly. "Benjamin?"

"Right." He held it up, and she slid her arms inside. When she turned around and faced him, he caught the lapels of her coat and smiled. "Ready?"

She nodded once and let out a breath. "Yep. Let's do this."

He offered his arm, and she took it. As they walked down the stairs of her brownstone, his driver opened the door. She smiled at him and slid inside, and Benjamin followed her. The second the door closed behind him, she sagged against the seat. The short ride to The Frick passed quickly, and in a few minutes, they were parked at the curb outside the hotspot.

Maggie sat up straight and pressed a hand to her stomach, turning green. "Oh God. We're here."

He reached for the door handle.

"Wait!" She pressed her hand even firmer against her stomach. "I'm allergic to shellfish. And I'm an only child. My roommate's name is Becca. And my parents—"

"—Are farmers in South Dakota. You have a black cat back home, who you rescued from an alley, and he hides when people come over so I'll probably never see him. His name is Lucifer. You also love the Yankees and the Giants, hate the Mets and the Jets, and you like long walks in a light, misting, rain." He cupped her cheek tenderly, smiling down at her reassuringly. "We've got this, darling."

She played with her seat belt, her fingers skittering over it nonstop. "You actually paid attention to all of that?"

"Of course I did. I want to learn everything about you, because I'm greedy when it comes to you. I won't pretend otherwise." He smoothed his thumb over her lower lip. "If you're talking? I'm listening. We've got this. There's nothing to worry about."

She straightened and nodded. "Okay. I'm ready."

"Sir?" The door opened, and his driver glanced down. "Madam?"

"Thank you, Jeff." He got out of the car and held his hand out. "Darling?"

She slid her hand into his. Her fingers didn't tremble.

There was a bit of a crowd checking their coats and greeting each other, but he didn't see his mother, so Maggie would be spared her company, at least for a little while. "She's not here yet."

"Good. I could use a drink or ten before taking her on." She pressed against his arm, her soft curves taunting him. "Think she upped her trash talk game yet? Or will she call me a 'lady of the night' again?"

He choked on a laugh, but managed to hold it back successfully. "I doubt she's ever actually uttered the word 'whore,' so I'd expect her trash talk to remain lame."

"Figures," Maggie muttered, checking out the hall. She held his arm tighter, hopping up and down excitedly. "Holy crap, is that a Kennedy over there? He's got the eyes and the hair."

He helped her out of her jacket. "Hmm? Where?"

"Over there." She shrugged free. "The short guy in black, next to the tall woman in black."

He rolled his eyes and laughed fully this time. "You realize that you just described everyone in the room, right?"

She shot him a frown over her shoulder. "That can't be true. Look—" She broke off, glanced around the room, and then down at her own gown, which was delightfully red. "Wait. Was I supposed to wear black? If so, I obviously missed the memo."

The red dress wasn't why she stood out in the crowd. She stood out because she was kind, gorgeous, and her laugh could light up an underground prison cell. "That's because there wasn't one. They're all dull, while you're full of life."

"But still." She nibbled on her lower lip. "Should I wear black next time?"

"Don't change a thing." He tipped her chin up. "I like you just the way you are."

A small smile slid into place. "You do?"

"I do."

He lowered his mouth to hers, brushing his mouth across hers in a short, sweet kiss. They were putting on a show for other people now, so he finally had an excuse to touch her. He damn well planned to enjoy it while it lasted. The taste of her remained after he pulled away, and it teased him, made him crave more instantly.

He had a feeling if he let himself, he could easily get addicted to her intoxicating taste. And not just *that*, but the way she made him laugh. He couldn't remember the last time he'd laughed at one of these boring affairs, yet he'd already done so twice tonight...

And they weren't even in the door yet.

"People were watching, so I figured it was a good time for a kiss," he whispered in her ear. Her fingers flexed on him, and she shivered. "For show only, of course."

"Y-Yes. Good thinking. We'll have to do that a lot tonight." She backed up a step. "I, uh, I see the bar, so I'm gonna get us some drinks while you check our coats. You want an old-fashioned?"

He cocked a brow. "Dare I ask how you found out I like those, darling?"

"Research," she said, twisting her purse. "Always research."

Spinning on her heel, she headed for the bar, looking every inch a regal princess amongst her peers. He watched her go, clasping the coats so tight his hands ached.

"Why, if it isn't Benjamin Gale the third," someone exclaimed from behind him. "It's been *so* long."

He stiffened. He'd recognize that voice anywhere. It was his latest ex—the one his mother had wanted him to marry. He'd refused because she reminded him of his mother. And he sure as hell didn't want to marry his mother. He'd rather marry Ivan the Terrible.

Forcing a pleasant expression even though the sound of her talking made him nauseated, he turned around. "Elizabeth. How wonderful to see you."

"I *know*." She beamed and rested a hand on his arm. Even her smile was icy. "Are you here alone, too? Oh, thank God. I have no one to dance with tonight, so this is perfect."

"Actually, I—"

"When your mother told me to come, and that you'd mentioned wanting to see me again, I didn't believe her. But now I'm here, and you're here, and this couldn't be more perfect." She rose up on tiptoe and pressed her cold lips to his cheek. "I've missed you, too. But you dreadfully need to shave."

He shook off her words. "My mother told you I missed you?"

"I did," his mother said from behind him. "I'm sorry if I betrayed your confidence, but I couldn't let it go. Not when you two are *so* well suited for one another."

"You couldn't be more right, Helen." Elizabeth curled her hand around his arm, clinging tightly and smiling at his mother. "We make a great couple. I've always thought so."

She pressed her slim frame against him as if to remind him what it felt like to be up close and intimate with her. He knew perfectly well how she felt—*wrong*.

She wasn't Maggie.

Chapter Ten

Maggie navigated the crowded hall slowly, watching the drinks in her hand cautiously. She'd opted for red wine, while getting Benji his old-fashioned. She smiled when she remembered his reaction when she'd asked him if he'd like one. The last time she'd gone to his penthouse, she'd talked to William for a few minutes. He was all too willing to impart information about his boss.

And she was *all* too willing to listen.

When it came to her fiancé, she was insatiable in her quest for knowledge. Despite all the romantic travesties in her past, and the fact that this whole affair would more than likely end in a disaster, she was going to give this a try.

She was going to give herself to Benji…

And stupidly hope for the best.

Someone bumped into her, but she managed to miraculously keep both drinks firmly in hand. She let out a sigh of relief and glanced up. It was the man she'd been watching earlier—and he was staring at her boobs. Not a Kennedy, then. Everyone knew they were ass men. "Sorry, Miss…?"

She did a little curtsy thing, since it was the best she could manage with full hands, and scanned the room, looking for Benjamin. She couldn't find him through the crowd. "Donovan. Maggie Donovan."

He bowed at the waist impatiently. "Lovely to meet you. Is that for me, sweetheart?"

"Is what for you?"

"The drink." He pointed at the old-fashioned in her left hand. "Whoever hired you, I'll pay double if you keep those coming."

"Uh..." He thought she was an assistant of some sort, or whatever. This was literally her worst nightmare about tonight, come to life. One glance, and the man somehow realized she wasn't one of them. Was it stamped across her forehead like a scarlett letter? "I'm not here as an assistant. This is for my fiancé. Maybe you know him?"

"Oh, so you're a...oh. Sorry. Uh... Fiancé?" He perked up and scratched his head. "Who might that be?"

"Benjamin Gale the third." Maggie smiled. "Of Gale Incorporated."

He straightened even more. "He's *engaged*? To you?" He gave her a once over, his mouth pressed into a thin line. "That can't be. You're not..."

He didn't finish that thought.

Probably because he didn't need to.

Tensing, she forced herself to keep smiling, to deny this jerk the satisfaction of seeing he'd shaken her. This was exactly the type of reception she'd expected, so she wasn't surprised. She'd said they would see through her deception with their X-ray vision and somehow figure out she wasn't blue-blooded like them.

And someone had. Already.

But deep down she'd hoped she could at least *pretend* to be one of them long enough that they'd actually believe she belonged here. "Yes, well, nonetheless, it's true. We're engaged." She tipped her head toward the door. "He's over there, checking our coats and waiting for me. So, if you'll excuse me?"

He laughed. "That's amusing."

"Oh?" she asked through clenched teeth. "How so?"

"Well, you see, he's over there with *my* daughter and his mother, Helen." He paused. "My daughter is his ex, who he is very much interested in making his 'future.' He informed her of as much just the other day. Ever since she left him, he hasn't been the same, you see."

Again. Neither the freaking meteorite nor the sinkhole showed up to save her.

What did a girl have to *do* to get a natural disaster around here?

Her heart skipped a beat or two, and she glanced to where she'd left Benjamin. Sure enough, he had a snobby-looking blonde on his arm, and he spoke with her and his mother…whose name was apparently *Helen*.

The blonde clung to him, and she rubbed her hand up and down his bicep as if she owned him already. While he didn't look a hundred percent at ease…

He didn't exactly look *upset*, either.

The sexy jerk.

Lifting her chin, she refused to react to the other man's words. "If you'll excuse me, I need to return to my fiancé and Helen. They'll be expecting me."

He stepped into her path. "Don't interfere with them. You have no idea what's at stake here."

"Oh, I have every idea what's at stake." She pushed past him. "It was lovely meeting you." *So freaking lovely.*

This time, he let her pass without stopping her.

As she crossed the room, the blonde pressed her bony body against Benjamin's and whispered something in his ear. Unexpected jealousy knifed through Maggie, hard and swift.

She wasn't supposed to be jealous…*was she*?

Sure, they'd kissed a few times, and he'd given her the best orgasm of her life without even trying, but the rest of their "relationship" was fake. They liked each other, and they were friends now, but that didn't mean he owed her anything—

Certainly not loyalty or fidelity.

And, hey, if he managed to find someone more suited to him to marry for real, someone who would keep his mother off his back for good, then more power to him. He deserved that, and more. But, even so, that didn't stop the jealousy from striking like lightning.

He glanced over the blonde's head, his attention locking on Maggie. Even from across the room, she could feel the question in his stare, as if he asked how she felt about this whole thing, or something. She forced a smile, lifted her wineglass to him, and downed it all in one gulp. Frowning, he said a few words to the two women and then came toward her without them.

His mother glowered at her, looking regal in her hatred.

Maggie smiled back and set her empty glass down, wiggling her fingers in a princess-like wave. *Game on, bitch.*

Her fiancé stepped into her path, blocking Helen's reaction. "What are you doing?" he hissed, grabbing her elbow. "Why didn't you come over?"

"You were busy." She lifted a shoulder. "And I didn't want to interfere."

He flexed his jaw. "The whole purpose of you being here is, in fact, to interfere in situations like this. It's why you're my fiancée, after all."

"Yeah, but then I figured out you were flirting with a former girlfriend, who you are still very much in love with, and from here…you looked quite content to be doing so." She crossed her arms. "I didn't want to mess things up if you were looking for a real solution to your problem, instead of a temporary one."

His dark blue eyes flashed angrily. "Is that so?"

"Yeah. That's so." She glanced over his shoulder. The blonde watched them closely, her lip caught between her teeth. "She's pretty. I bet she'd be a good wife. I didn't want to ruin your chances by coming up and acting like I was the one you really wanted on you arm, when we both know—"

"You obviously know nothing." He dragged his hand through his hair. "If I wanted to marry her, I wouldn't have broken up with her in the first place. And you *are* the one I really want by my side. I made that perfectly clear the other night, when I said we'd take it slow and see where things went, but that I hoped they'd go somewhere with us naked in bed together. I was pretty fucking clear what I wanted."

"Look, it's fine if—" She stopped midsentence. "Wait, *you* broke up with *her*?"

"You're damn right I did." He dropped his hand to his side. "So next time, instead of writing a whole damn story in your head, just come the hell over. If I don't want to be interrupted, I'll wave you off. But you can pretty safely assume I want you to come up and show whoever I'm talking to that I'm taken."

The jealousy that had been turning Maggie a wicked shade of green faded away, and she smiled while setting down his untouched drink. She could feel his mother's glare burning into them both, as well as the blonde's *and* her father's.

Time to give them a show.

Resting her hands on his chest, she smoothed his tuxedo. "You mean, I should do something..." Stepping closer, she lifted her chin and studied his mouth. The wine she'd chugged earlier hit, and the room spun a little bit as she pressed her body up against his. Maybe this wasn't the best of ideas, but she was past caring. "...more like this, next time?"

He cocked a brow and grasped her hips. "Yeah."

"More than a touch? A kiss, maybe?"

She didn't give him a chance to say anything that might dissuade her from showing that blonde exactly who Benjamin was with—real or not. Rising up on tiptoe, which was a lot easier with heels on, she kissed him in front of everyone. For a second, he hesitated, almost as if he was going to pull away, but instead he moaned and crushed her to his chest. His mouth moved over hers, and he kissed her back with abandon.

Swept up in a feeling that was anything but just for show, she closed her fists on his tuxedo jacket, hanging on for dear life. He broke the kiss off and let out a shaky breath. *"Maggie."*

She bit down on her lower lip. She still tasted him on her. "Yes, Benji?"

Pressing his mouth against her ear, he tugged her closer. His huge erection pressed against her belly, and he whispered, "When we leave here later and get to your apartment, you'll have a choice. If you invite me in, I swear you'll never doubt your welcome in my arms again, and you'll see exactly how much I want you."

A shiver swept over her, and she didn't let go. She wouldn't have been able to even if she tried. "Benjamin…"

"Yeah. I know. It's a bad idea." His nostrils flared. "Let's go mingle. The sooner we get this night over with, the better."

"How long do we have to stay?"

A muscle ticked in his jaw, and he grabbed the drink off the table. He swallowed it in one big gulp then set it down. "Until they all see us, and realize we're engaged."

He offered his arm, and she held him close to her body, stealing a quick glance up at him. His offer burned in her mind. Even if they only had a short romance, what was so wrong with seizing the moment…

And having a little fun with a man she was desperately

attracted to?

She caught her breath, because if she did this, went through with fulfilling her desire, it would change everything. Tonight would decide how the rest of their relationship went, real or fake. Would she play it safe, like always, and tell him she wanted to remain friends? Or would she let him in, even though she shouldn't?

Guess she was about to find out because, despite her inner voice jumping up and down and screaming *no...*

She wanted to invite him in.

Chapter Eleven

The night had been one tedious conversation after another, followed by endless snide remarks about his engagement to someone no one had ever heard of. Not even the open bar had helped dull the monotonous company. If one good thing had come of tonight, it had been Maggie.

She'd handled the night with grace and even managed to win over a few of the older members of society while she'd been at it. The younger ones had been too busy judging them from afar to actually talk to her, but if they were too blind to see how special she was, that was their loss.

After that odd encounter with his ex, and Maggie's even odder reaction to it, the night had been fairly hiccup free. She had remained by his side the whole evening, and the few times she'd wandered off, she hadn't hesitated to come right back and claim him as her own. Repeatedly. He was proud to call her his.

Even if she thought it was only for pretend.

In the car on the ride home, she shifted in her seat and fidgeted with her purse. She'd been a nervous mess ever since they pulled away from The Frick, probably because of what he'd said after that kiss he couldn't stop thinking about. That had been on him. She wasn't ready, but when she'd kissed him like that, he'd forgotten all about rules and patience. He *wanted* her. She wanted him, too.

Sometimes, when her soft lips were pressed to his and her hands were on him, it was hard to remember that she didn't *want* to want him. That for her, it was all for show.

It killed him that he had to play it safe with her, when all he wanted to do was grab her, kiss her, and show her exactly how well the two of them would fit together. He'd never fought this hard to get a woman before, but the thing was, he didn't even mind. She was worth every second he spent trying to prove she should trust him.

She might want him, but she wouldn't act on those impulses, because she "knew" how it would end. He disagreed. She was all rational thought and consequences, and he had to respect that. No matter how badly he ached to make her cry out his name again…

With more than just his fucking *knee*.

He sat forward and rested his elbows on his thighs. "You did great tonight, darling."

She startled before turning to him. The force of those gray eyes of hers stole the rest of his words out of his mouth. Her hair looked even softer than it had earlier, and he ached to touch it. "Thanks. I think it went fairly well."

"It did." He smiled. "Thank you, again, for doing this. There are more exciting ways to spend your nights than with snobs who have nothing better to do with their lives than gossip about everyone else's."

"It's fine. I didn't mind doing it…for you."

That's what made her so unique. His fingers itched to touch her, to show her just how special she made him feel, but he didn't move a damn muscle. He'd already crossed the line once tonight, when he misinterpreted her kiss to mean she wanted something more. Mistaking her intentions twice would be unacceptable.

When the car stopped outside her apartment, he got out and walked around to her side, waving his driver off. He could damn well open the door for the woman who had done so much for him, in such a short time, and asked for nothing in return.

Once she stood on the sidewalk, hugging herself, he closed the door. "I'll pick you up tomorrow at five for Rockefeller Center, and then two on Sunday for the theatre."

"Okay." She hesitated, not moving toward her stairs. "Look, about earlier, when I kissed you, and you said—"

He held a hand up. "I got caught up in the moment. You made it quite clear you want to keep this thing between us platonic, and I shouldn't have pushed for more."

"But—"

He locked eyes with her. "I'm sorry, and I take it back. All of it."

"Okay." She nibbled on her lower lip. "Well, then…good night, I guess."

He inclined his head. "Good night."

She still didn't move.

Neither did he.

The tension built between them, fast and thick. If this were any other woman, he'd think she wanted him to kiss her, but she'd made it pretty damn clear she didn't want that at all. But, holy shit, he did.

"Do you want to come in?" she finally asked. "Have a drink?"

Yes. *Hell* yes. "I do. But if I come in there, I'm following through on every promise I've made, and you'll be screaming my name within the hour."

She cocked her head. "Is that a promise?"

"Damn right it is, which is why I should leave." He reached out and grasped her chin, unable to resist. "You're not ready, darling. I shouldn't have pushed you earlier."

She shrugged, still clinging to her purse as if it could save her. They stared at one another, the tension mounting even higher than his heart rate. It was as if she silently asked him to do something—*anything*. What? He had no idea. He didn't speak "woman."

"Like I said..." She tugged on her hair. "Wanna come in?"

He'd resisted the first time. He wouldn't be able to do so twice. "Hell yeah."

He waved his driver off and followed her up the stairs. Her hips swung with each step, as if she sought to torture him with the very thing he couldn't have, since she'd more than likely change her mind before he could kiss her. And yet he followed her inside anyway because he was a masochistic asshole like that.

She flicked the lights on and glanced over her shoulder. "Beer?"

"Sure," he said, shrugging out of his coat. He laid it across the chair where she'd dropped hers. "Thanks."

She went into the kitchen, and he wandered around the living room. The picture on the shelf above the sofa was askew, so he nudged it straight before settling on the couch. She had a bunch of photos of herself with what he could only assume were her parents, a few of her with her roommate, but none of them had men in them.

He wasn't sure *why* that made him happy, but it did.

When she came back into the living room carrying two open beers, he smiled at her. She kicked off her heels but still wore her dress, and was as gorgeous as always. He took the beer she offered him, and copied her, taking his shoes off and sliding them side by side under the table with his foot.

She sat down beside him, turning toward him and tucking her foot under her. Her knee touched his thigh, and he stiffened. Resting her head on a hand, she leaned against the back of the couch and smiled at him. "So…"

He raised a brow. "So?"

"How do you think tomorrow—?" She broke off, pressed her lips together, and shook her head. "You know what? Screw this."

After setting down her beer, she yanked his out of his hand mid sip. He blinked. "Hey. I was drinking that.

"I'm done." She straddled his lap and cupped his face. His heart lurched, and his cock thickened with need. "I invited you in. Now it's time for you to fulfill your part of the bargain, Benji."

He held her still, digging his fingers into her thighs, but didn't move. "Say it. I need to hear you say it."

"Kiss me. Take me." She buried her hands securely in his hair. "Make me yours."

"I thought you'd never ask," he said, sliding his hands down her legs, and back up—only this time under her skirt. "*Maggie*."

He kissed her fully. All the other times they'd kissed, minus the time he'd made her come, he'd held himself back. Hadn't let himself get caught up in the moment. Well, not this time.

This time, he was all fucking in.

She gasped and clung to him, rolling her hips against him hungrily. He entwined his tongue with hers, loving the way she tasted. Hell, she tasted like she was his—and he liked that. He slid his hands up her curves. If he was a poetic man, he could write a verse or two about the way her waist flared out slightly at her hips, intoxicating him. He arched up, rubbing against her warm core, and she moaned, pressing down firmly.

She broke the kiss off and drew in a ragged breath. "I need a minute...I need..."

He brushed her hair out of her face. "I've made many mistakes in my life, but this isn't one of them." He picked her up and laid her down on the couch, lowering his body over hers. "You never know what life will throw at you, or how things will go, but this isn't a mistake. And you sense that, too, which is what scares you so much."

He kissed her again, gently, and after a moment of hesitation, she kissed him back, wrapping her legs and arms around him. That was all the answer he needed. *This*.

Skimming his fingers up her soft thigh, he cupped her ass, hauling her closer to him as he deepened the kiss. She gasped and dug her nails into his shoulders, her tongue circling his. Something that felt this good, this *right*, couldn't be wrong.

And he refused to believe it could be.

Smoothly, he stood and picked her up without breaking her hold on him, or their kiss. He headed for the hallway to the left, where she'd come from earlier. When he pushed through the door, he strode to the bed in the middle of the room, tossed her on it and yanked his bowtie off.

There was a meow, a hiss, and claws scratching against wood as her cat bolted out of the room. "Oops."

A laugh escaped her, and he joined her as he dropped his bowtie to the floor. And it felt fucking amazing to be undressing a woman and laughing over something as silly as a damn *cat*.

"Don't worry about him. He was just hiding under the bed, like usual." She watched him closely, licking her lips and pressing her thighs together. It was, hands down, the most erotic thing he'd ever seen. Just like that, his mood shifted from amused to unquenchable lust for Maggie. "Close the door," she said.

Crossing the room, he did as told. "Protection?" he

managed to grit out.

"Oh, right." She rolled over and opened the drawer next to her bed. Taking out a foil packet, she tossed it at him. "There you go."

He undid the buttons of his shirt, and she lifted herself up on elbows. When his shirt was off, he grabbed his waistband, uncertain whether he should take his pants off or not. *She* hadn't removed a single article of clothing yet.

"Benjamin," she said, her voice coming out a little bit strangled "I...I want to see you. All of you. Don't stop."

He bit back a moan. He planned on making her say that again, later, louder. And naked. Not wasting time, he flicked his wrist and let his pants hit the floor.

Her breath came in short bursts, her chest rising and falling in short bursts. "You're...you're not wearing any underwear."

He cocked a brow. "Your turn. Take. It. *Off.*"

She rose up on her knees, turning her back to him. He studied her for any signs of hesitation. As much as he wanted her, he needed to make sure she wouldn't regret this. Wouldn't regret *him*. "Unzip me?"

He swallowed hard, stepping closer. Gently, he pushed her hair over her shoulder, exposing the nape of her neck. Leaning down, he kissed the spot directly above her spine. "You're so pretty." He unzipped a bit, and kissed the skin he bared. "So soft." Some more, and another kiss halfway down her spine. "So sweet." He hit the bottom of the zipper and pushed the dress off her shoulder. This time, instead of a kiss, he nipped the skin at the small of her back. "So *mine*."

Shuddering, she faced him, holding her dress on at the shoulders. After taking a deep breath, she let go, and he staggered back. Actually *staggered* back. The swell of her hips was the sexiest thing he'd ever seen, and he couldn't look away. Her large breasts were encased in a sheer black bra, and her panties were pretty much nonexistent.

That was somehow even sexier than no panties at all.

"Jesus," he gritted out, grabbing a hold of her and flipping her onto her back. "You're perfect. Unbelievably gorgeous. And unbelievably *sexy*."

She gasped and arched her back, digging her nails into the comforter beneath her. "Benjamin. I need… I need…"

"Me. You need me." He nipped right above her knee, swirling his tongue over the love bite to sooth the sting. She hissed in a breath, writhing against him. "Say it, Maggie."

"You," she breathed. "I need you *now*." She cupped her core, shooting him the naughtiest look he'd ever seen. "Here."

When she bit her lip and rolled her hips, touching herself, he laid his hand over hers, stilling her fingers. He was all too happy to give her what she wanted. He kissed a slow path up her thigh, slowing even more when he neared her barely there lingerie, and she struggled to move her fingers underneath his.

Arching her hips up, she threaded her free hand in his hair. He inhaled deeply. She smelled like heaven. "Ben… *please*." She lifted herself up. "I need you."

He removed her hand, tore her thong off, and tossed it over his shoulder. Groaning, he ran his fingers over her small patch of soft brown curls, and over her clit. She cried out, spreading her legs more for him. And what a pretty picture she was. All swollen lips, pink skin, and desire.

Leaning in, he flicked his tongue over her, sliding his hands under her perfect ass to lift her up. She cried out and closed her thighs around his head. "Oh my—*yes*. Benjamin. *Yes*."

He closed his mouth over her, swirling his tongue in wide, gentle circles. His cock begged to be buried inside her, but it would have to wait. First, she had to scream, cry, and *plead*. She had to need him, damn it.

Like *he* needed *her*.

Chapter Twelve

Benjamin was going to *kill* her. He kept teasing her with soft caresses of his tongue, then he'd pull back so she couldn't come and start all over again. If he kept it up, he might find out what it felt like to be punched by a farmer's daughter. She had a strong uppercut, thanks to her father's tutelage, so he'd be surprised.

Then again, maybe he wouldn't be.

He seemed to understand her better than any other man she'd ever been with, and it was kind of scary. Cool, too, but mostly frightening. She kept pushing him away, but he hadn't let her drive him off, like she had other men. And he was right. What they had together *did* feel like it was meant to be, which made this whole mess even worse, because they didn't stand a chance of making it.

But she was going to do it anyway.

And he'd be with her the whole time.

He ran his thumb over her clitoris, watching her as she tensed—and then he did it *again*. "*Yes*."

"I love it when you make that sound," he said, lifting his

head from between her thighs. Lucky for him, he showed no signs of retreating. If he had, she would've jammed her heel into his upper back till he finished what he started. "So sexy."

He flicked his tongue over her again, and she cried out, so close to the edge it hurt. All she needed was one last push and she'd be flying, soaring, floating. He dug his fingers into her skin and deepened his intimate kiss, and she got what she needed. She came explosively, and the whole world froze around them.

Everything ceased to exist except this. Them. What he made her feel.

And it was incredible.

"*Maggie*," he said, his voice broken and raw.

He let her hit the mattress and grabbed the condom off the side of the bed. While he rolled it on with steady fingers, she looked her fill. She'd always thought he couldn't possibly look any hotter than he did in his business suits, but she was wrong. He was ridiculously hot out of them, too.

So not fair.

His broad shoulders and hard pecs narrowed down to an admirable six-pack, and he had a heck of an erection, too. So much so that she wondered if the condom would even work for him because *oh my God, he was huge.*

He *really* had it all.

He lowered his body over hers again and kissed her, his tongue seeking and finding hers as he slid his hands behind her back and undid her bra without a struggle. When he closed his palms over her breasts, dragging his thumb over her aching nipples, she moaned into his mouth. When he did it again, even rougher, the same broken sound escaped her.

Breaking off the kiss, he rested his forehead on hers, his breathing uneven and harsh. His hard length pressed against her, close but not close enough. Nothing would ever be close enough. "I'm trying to take it slow. To make love to you slowly, but damn it, I need you, darling."

"Then stop trying." She dug her heels into the muscles of his butt. "Go slow next time."

"Next time," he uttered almost reverently, as if he couldn't believe he'd get one. As if this was a one and done deal. Maybe that was all he wanted, and she'd just made a fool of herself by assuming he'd want more. He touched her cheek softly, eyeing her with a possessive strength that took her breath away. "Yeah."

"Unless you don't want—"

"Oh, I want." He buried his face in her neck. "I fucking want."

And then he thrust inside of her in one long, hard motion.

She dug her nails into his back, closing her eyes. Biting down on her shoulder, he moved his hips in a way that made her think she'd died and gone to heaven, because the things he did to her weren't possible.

Nothing real could feel *that* good.

He pulled almost all the way out of her and then drove back in, hitting some magical, mythical spot she'd only ever read about, but never felt. She wanted to shy away from it, because it was *so* out of her control, and that scared her, but she couldn't fight it.

Couldn't fight him.

She arched her back, dragging her nails down his arms. "*Benjamin.*"

"Shh. I'm here, Maggie. I have you." He lifted her hips. "Hold on tight, darling. I promise I won't let go."

He caught her mouth with his and drove even deeper.

She clung to him, no longer fighting the feelings he brought out in her. Tension pooled in her stomach, drowning out everything. All that remained was what he was doing to her, sweeping her into an inferno of passion and pleasure until she was weak.

"*Jesus.*" He grunted and moved harder, faster, and smoother inside of her, his hands flexing on her butt. "You feel…too…fucking…good. Addicting."

She wanted to reply, she *really* did.

But all she could manage was a strangled groan that came out more like a sob. The tension building inside her tightened, and every nerve in her body tingled, until she was sure something had to give or she'd die. He kissed her again, thrusting inside her, and slid his hand between them to press against her clitoris.

She screamed into his mouth, stars bursting in front of her as she came stronger than she'd *ever* come before. The second she flew into the sky, he tensed, too, and his whole body stiffened. He let out a string of curses and collapsed on top of her, his heart thumping against hers. She wrapped her arms around him, hugging him close even though she shouldn't. He didn't move away.

If anything, he snuggled closer.

After a few minutes, he let out a long sigh. "Jesus, Maggie." He lifted up on his elbows and stared down at her, his blue eyes somehow darker and stormier than she'd ever seen them. "That was fucking incredible."

She smiled at him shyly, loving how he lost himself in her arms enough to let the f-bomb fly without apologizing. "It was."

He smoothed her hair and smiled back at her tenderly. Like, really smiled at her. Dimples and all. Even his eyes shone with happiness. His smiles always stole her breath away, but this time he did more than that. He stole her soul, too, like some sort of ninja. "Still think I'm the worst mistake you ever made?" he asked.

Her head was spinning, and she was a mess of emotions, confusion, and a little bit of fear. "Nope."

"Progress." He kissed her lightly, pulling back way too

soon. He was still smiling, and his eyes were still unguarded. "Good."

She ran her fingers over his hard biceps and glanced away. "But it doesn't have to change anything if you don't want it to. This could happen again, or it could be a one time only thing, and we go back to being friends." The more she spoke, the stiffer he got on top of her. Yet she kept on talking because once she started, she couldn't stop. It was like a verbal bomb exploded inside her. "I don't expect anything out of you at all, just because you saw me naked. I'm one hundred percent okay with going back to the way things were, if that's what you want."

"Are you now? How *great* to know." He rolled off her and rested a hand on his flat stomach. His jaw flexed as he stared up at the ceiling at nothing in particular. He seemed so closed right now, with no emotion whatsoever showing on his face, so she had no idea what was going through his head. Like freaking usual. "I get it. You've been hurt by some jackass before. But I'm not that guy."

"I know you're not him." She swallowed and fought the urge to cover herself with something. Talking about something so vulnerable while being so, well, *naked*, was not her idea of fun. She played with a piece of her hair and pursed her lips, trying to pretend like it wasn't awkward at all to be talking to her boss-slash-fake fiancé-slash-real lover, while naked no less, about her poor life choices. So she let out a nervous laugh. "You could say I don't exactly have the best track record with men, like, ever. At all."

He rubbed his chin and turned to her. She stared up at her ceiling fan, which wasn't even moving. "Have you ever loved anyone?" he asked.

"Wow," she said, laughing uneasily again. She tugged on a piece of hair and wrapped it around her finger, fighting the panic rising in her chest. Where the heck was he going with this? She couldn't think of a single reason why he'd ask her that. "Deep talk. Are you sure we're ready for this? I mean, we literally *just* finished having sex for the first time."

"I think it's a great time, because you said that you didn't think I was a mistake." He rolled off the bed, walked over to the trash can, disposed of the condom, and then picked up his pants. After stepping into them, he buttoned and zipped them up, and smoothed his hair. He looked unbelievably, undeniably, hot as hell. "After which you immediately tried to run away."

"I didn't run." She held her hands out. "I didn't even get out of *bed*."

"Doesn't mean you weren't running." He frowned at her, catching her gaze and refusing to let go. "You're pushing me away again, just like you do every time I get too close to you. It's getting really fucking old, Maggie."

Had she done that?

Yeah, okay. She kind of had, but it wasn't an intentional slight.

It was just…habit.

In her experience, once men got what they wanted—*aka* sex—they were done with you. She'd given him that, so it was only a matter of time till he left, or did something drastically horrible to ruin everything.

It's what men did.

Especially the ones she dated.

"I'm sorry," she said. It wasn't enough, but it was true. "I didn't mean to do that. To hurt you."

He didn't reply, just rolled his hands into tight fists. She knew she'd messed up everything with her knee jerk reaction to the way he made her feel, so she swallowed hard and stared at the fan again. It was safer than looking at *him*. It didn't offer much distraction, but she did notice she needed to dust it. And—

He let out an irritated sound. "*Look* at me."

She fisted the comforter underneath of her and slowly turned to him, as he'd requested. He wasn't naked anymore, while she was, and it felt weird.

Sitting up, she hugged her knees, trying to shield herself in more ways than one. "What do you want from me, Benjamin?"

"You. Just you." He must've read something in her expression, because he picked up her robe and tossed it at her. She caught it easily. "You say one thing, and then do another, and I have no damn clue what you want from me. You've been hurt before, and you're scared to risk letting another man in. But you've got to *try*, or we don't stand a chance in hell of making it outside this room. Can you do that? Can you let me in?"

Her throat throbbed, and she could feel tears looming. Not because she was upset or in pain, but because he got her. Like, really *got* her, and that was both frightening and enlightening all at once. She shrugged into her robe and hugged it closed. "You're right. I am scared. But that's because I see how—"

"How this ends," he finished.

She swallowed hard. "Yeah."

"*Bullshit*." He dragged his hand through his hair and sat beside her. Reaching out, he caught both her hands in his. "You can't know how something is going to end before it even begins. It's not humanly possible."

"I think it began a while ago, so it's not too hard to understand what comes next."

"So what happens now?" He squeezed her fingers. "Go on. Tell me."

She lifted a shoulder. "You got what you wanted, so you leave."

He let her go. "Excuse me?"

"Sex." She bit her tongue. "You got it, and now you'll move on."

"Is that really what you think of me?" he asked quietly. He sounded...hurt. She turned to him. His blue eyes were dark and haunted. "Do you think I fucked you, and now I'm finished with you? Just like that?"

"Not to hurt me, or anything. It's not anything personal. It's just..." She bit her lip. "It's how guys are. I get it."

"Jesus, Maggie." His jaw tightened and he shook his head, picking up his shirt angrily. The muscles in his arm were hard and the veins stuck out. "I had no idea you had such a poor opinion of me."

"It's not you," she said quickly. Tightening her fingers on her knees, she tried to think how best to get him to understand what she meant. "It's me."

He laughed. "Wow. I've never had that used on me before."

"N-No. I'm not breaking it off with you. That's not what I'm saying."

"What the fuck do you want, Maggie?" He held his arms out. "You want me to stay, or to go? Care, or not care? Tell me what you want, and it's yours."

She wrung her hands. It was all or nothing. She had to open up, and let him in, and hope he didn't make her regret it. "I want you to stay, to care, but that scares me. It scares me *a lot*."

"Why?" He white-knuckled his shirt. "Because I'm such an uncaring beast?"

"You're right. Because every time I've let someone into my heart, all it's done is given him a weapon to use against me. And nine times out of ten? He used that weapon."

"Who used the weapon on you, Maggie?"

"Who didn't?" She lifted a shoulder. It wasn't easy to talk about this, but he deserved the truth. "I told you about one of my exes, but what you don't realize is they've *all* hurt me.

They've all done horrible things. The one before the last one not only broke my heart, he tore it to shreds. Slept with my best friend back home, right in front of me, but I was too stupid to notice. And when I finally did see it? He didn't even stop. Just invited me to join. She laughed at me. So did he. The guy before him *literally* stole from me. My wallet. My TV. All of it."

Benjamin sat down, watching her. "I'm not that kind of guy."

"Maybe not. But there have been other guys like him. Every man I've trusted with my heart has broken it. Broken me or *robbed* me." She tapped her fingers on her thighs restlessly, because she'd just bared her soul, and it scared her more than he did. "So, I don't let myself care anymore. I push people away before they get close enough to hurt me. But with you, it's harder than usual. I *want* to care. I *want* to let you in. That's the God's honest truth."

"Maggie…" he said, his face closed off.

She laughed lightly. "And the worst part is, I can never tell what you're thinking. You say you need me with one breath, but with the next you act as if you wouldn't even blink if I left you. I can't freaking read you."

For a few seconds, he didn't move, didn't acknowledge her words at all. She thought he would leave without answering. But he dropped his shirt and climbed back into the bed. Cupping her face, he smiled at her gently. He didn't look anything like the beast that had once roamed the halls of the office, looking for prey.

"I can usually read your reactions," he said, "but I can't predict them ahead of time. And that's new for me. So we're both in uncharted territory, here. And I don't like to let people in, either. I don't really know how. No one ever let me in, so I didn't want to, either."

She pressed her lips together. "And yet you want me to do it for you?"

"Because I'm doing it for you." He let out a long breath. "With you, I drop all my acts and pretenses. I'm the real me. The one I've become so good at hiding. Gales don't show emotion. It's just not done. And once my dad died, I stopped. I've been trying to be this person I'm not, but around you—I can be *me*, Maggie. You have no idea how fucking good that feels." He ran his thumb over her jaw. "But I'm not trying to hurt you, and I don't want a *weapon* to use against you. If you trust me, and let me in, I swear not to use that against you. That's the last thing I'd do. I want to make you happy, not sad."

Her heart lurched, and she swallowed hard, finally locking gazes with him. "Benjamin..."

"Let me try something." He closed his eyes, and when he looked at her again...she forgot to breathe. What she saw there was honesty, and *happiness*. For the first time, he opened himself up to her. "There. I'm letting you in too, see? So we both have a weapon in our hands, ready to strike or lay down on the floor. What do you say about that?"

Her heart raced. It was time to let go of the past hurts and to trust Benjamin. Time to take a chance again. Wrapping her fingers around his wrists, she nodded once. "Drop it on the floor."

"Done." His hold on her tightened. "What about you? Will you stop pushing me away every time I get too close?"

"Yes." She bit her lip. "I promise."

Grinning, he wrapped her in his arms and rolled her beneath him. Her heart thudded against her ribs, hard and quick, and he slid his hand under her butt. "I won't make you sorry. I swear it."

He kissed her, and she clung to that statement, and to the way he made her feel. For the first time in years she let herself hope that something as impossible as a happy ending between the two of them could happen. And she didn't let go.

She took a *chance*.

Chapter Thirteen

Two days later, the town car pulled up in front of the Richard Rogers Theatre, and Benjamin stole a glance at Maggie. After their talk the other night, they made love again, and he held her till she fell asleep. And amazingly enough, he'd spent the night, too.

And he hadn't let her go.

The next night, they went to a gala, and she did great. His mother hadn't been at that one, so for the most part they were able to relax and enjoy one another—she even made a few friends. Elizabeth had been there again, but she hadn't had a chance to get him alone. She'd simply stared from a distance, her icy blue glare zeroed in on Maggie.

She had barely noticed, though. She'd been too busy dazzling everyone around her...including *him*. The more time Benjamin spent with her, the more sure he became of the decision he'd made when he'd begged—yes, he wasn't too proud to admit he'd begged—her to let him in. This feeling he had in his gut, the one that wouldn't go away no matter how hard he tried to shove it down?

He had an inkling what it would turn into given time, if he let it.

It was too soon to be sure, but this feeling was strong, and could really become something huge. Life changing. He should probably be worried about that, or at least a little bit apprehensive about taking something fake and turning it into something real, but he wasn't.

It felt *right*.

Maggie picked up her purse and held it to her chest. She wore a soft pink dress, and a pair of black heels. Her hair was swept to the side, with loose strands escaping to frame her face. Effortlessly beautiful, as always. "What are we seeing, again? I can't remember."

"I forget the name, but it's a show about choices. It's off Broadway now, but it's a special performance for charity." He opened the door and climbed out into the brisk night. "It's about a woman and the way two parallel lives play out based on a decision she makes in the beginning of the show."

She slid her hand into his and let him help her out onto the sidewalk. "Wow, okay."

"What?"

"Well, it just kind of reminds me of the other night at my place. That was a pretty big choice Friday night, right?" She shot him a nervous smile, as if uncertain of her words. "We both decided to take this thing we have, roll with it, and hope for the best."

He swallowed hard and squeezed her fingers. "Yeah, we did, didn't we?"

Something flashed across her expression, and for once he couldn't read it. "I—"

"Well, look who it is. The happy lovebirds," his mother said from behind him. "How...*sweet*."

She obviously found it anything but, though that didn't take rocket science to figure out. She'd spent all weekend leaving him messages that told him exactly how much she disliked his choice of fiancée.

Oh-the-fuck-well.

Maggie made him happy, and for once that was all he was going to worry about. His mother wanted him to settle down and become serious with someone, so fine. He had. If she didn't like who he picked, too damn bad.

"Mother." He turned and embraced her, kissing her temple, like she'd instructed him to do as soon as he was old enough to show "love" properly in public. She patted his back, like always. "How lovely to see you. No one told me you were coming."

"It was a last minute decision." She eyed Maggie, and he could practically hear her calculating all her weaknesses, and figuring out where it would be best to strike. It was what she did. Who she was. Who he'd been, too—until Maggie showed him a different way. "Your brother had an extra ticket."

He threw his arm around Maggie's shoulder protectively. "Lovely."

"Yes, that's how Andrew is." She finally looked away from Maggie and gave him a hard stare. "Always sharing what he has with those he cares about."

"Benjamin." Andrew came up behind her as if on cue. "Good to see you."

"Hey." He hugged his brother before stepping back to Maggie's side. He entwined fingers with her. "We missed you at the gala last night," Benjamin said.

"Something came up last minute." He side-eyed their mother, who remained impassively still, then he turned to Maggie. "You must be Ms. Donovan."

"Maggie." She offered a hand. "And you must be the brother I've heard so much about. You work in the other Gale Incorporated office downtown, right?"

Andrew bowed over her hand. "Indeed."

"It's lovely meeting you," she said, smiling.

"Likewise." Andrew grinned back. "Let me introduce you to my wife. She's over there, in black."

"Of course she is," Maggie said softly. "I'd love to meet her."

"I'll wait here," Benjamin said, reluctantly letting go of her hand.

Maggie and Andrew wandered off together, and he watched them go. If she showed any signs of needing rescue, he'd be at her side in two seconds flat.

But he had a feeling she'd be fine. His brother wasn't the enemy.

His mother sighed and shifted on her feet impatiently, reminding him of who was. "I assume you got my messages, Benjamin? All twenty-six of them?"

"I did." He tugged on his tie. "Sorry, we've been busy socializing all weekend, and introducing Maggie to everyone, so I didn't have a chance to return your calls."

"How delightful," she said drily. "I'm sure they all *adore* her."

"They do," he said defensively.

"Did you listen to my messages at all?" She switched her purse to her other hand, her motions jerky. "Obviously, you didn't. After all, she remains at your side, despite my numerous warnings."

And that was what annoyed her the most. That she couldn't control him. It wouldn't work this time, and that *killed* her.

Maggie spoke with Andrew quietly, so Benjamin finally glanced away and gave his mother his full attention. "Oh, I heard every word. You wanted me to settle down. I did. I found a woman who makes me happy, and now you want me to leave her and find someone that doesn't. Does that sum it up?"

"Happy?" She let out a dainty snort. "What a silly, fleeting concept."

"I used to think so, too. But then I met her." Maggie glanced over and gave him a small smile. He smiled back. "And I saw how wrong I was."

"You're actually serious," she said, horror tingeing her voice. "About this...this...*woman*?"

"Dead serious." He tugged on his jacket sleeves so they hit at the same exact spot on his wrists. "Funny how life works, huh? Right when you decided you'd had enough of me being single, I met her, and fell in love. It all just kind of works out."

She made a small sound. "She is *not* acceptable. You need to marry someone of good breeding. Someone like Elizabeth. Someone who can bring something to the table besides her skills in the bedroom."

"Don't talk about her like that," he snapped, fighting the urge to tell his mother to piss off—and stay the hell out of his life. He watched Maggie charm his brother and sister-in-law, and forced a calm breath. "I'm not with her because of anything she gives me. I'm with her because she makes me happy. And because I adore her."

"Even if that's true, what can she possibly offer you in return?"

"Herself. Just herself." He uncurled his fists. "Turns out that's all I need. Now, if you'll excuse me?"

His mother stepped in front of him, cutting Maggie off from his line of sight. "Don't be a fool. Settling down with a woman like her is as good as not settling down at all. I didn't fight as hard as I did, for as long as I did, to keep your inheritance intact, only to watch you squander it away on a gold digger. Pick someone with an appropriate background, or I'll do everything in my power to unseat you as CEO. And I swear to God, I *will win*."

What had happened to her to make her so bitter? So jaded? He'd asked her once, but she had looked down her nose at him, huffed, and said, *life*. "Andrew doesn't even want my job. He told me so." He shoved his hands into his pockets and forced a calm expression. "Your threats are empty, Mother. You have no play to make here, so I'm calling your bluff. The truth is, I just don't believe you anymore."

"Why do you think Andrew was with me last night, then, if he's not 'interested'?" She laughed. "You foolish boy. I had the highest paid members of the board, their wives, *and* your brother over for dinner last night—while you were playing house with that woman."

His gut clenched tight, making him feel sick to his stomach. "What?"

"The motion has already begun. I'd hoped to knock some sense into you, but if you insist on this foolhardy plan to marry someone without a penny to her name…you'll be finished. Ruined." She crossed her arms. "And you'll have no one to blame but yourself."

He stepped back, unable to believe she'd actually initiated the no confidence vote against him. Her own *son*. "Why do you hate me so much?"

"I told you I was willing to do what needs to be done to protect the things I care about the most," she said, ignoring his question. "I refuse to watch you ruin the company to which I dedicated my whole life, because you found a woman who makes you *happy*."

The things she *cared* about. He, obviously, was not one of them.

"Why is being happy so damn bad? Actually, never mind." He laughed, an angry, bitter noise. His mother wasn't just upset with him, or disappointed in him for his failure. No, she *hated* him. Actually *hated* him. "What kind of mother are you?"

She lifted her chin. "The kind who will stop at nothing to win. What kind of son are you? Oh, dear. We already know the answer to that, don't we? You're a wastrel and a scoundrel who is too busy to come to his dying father's bedside."

That stung like a bitch, and the all too familiar cloak of guilt suffocated him, choking the breath out of his lungs. "Wow. Guess the gloves are off now."

"They've been off," she admitted, smoothing her short brown hair. "You've just never noticed before."

He took a step closer, anger rising inside of him like an unstoppable tidal wave. "I've done nothing but try to make this company my life. To try to make up for not being there. I've never wavered from doing my best for the company, and I am one hundred percent committed to the success of my father's life work, even if I didn't..." He shook his head slowly. "I was practically a kid when he died. You can't hold that against me for the rest of my life."

Maggie wrapped up her talk with Andrew, shook hands with Sarah, and made her way over to him, smiling and waving. He lifted a hand in reply.

"I can, and I will." His mother noticed and stepped closer, lowering her voice, but not answering his question. "You have until Monday night to lose the girl. If you don't, I'll move forward on my motion. Enjoy the show."

She walked over to Andrew, completely ignored Maggie as she passed, then smiled and hugged her favorite son. Anger, pain, and shock rocked him hard. His mother was always threatening shit, but this was the first time she'd actually gone so far as to get things moving, or actually given him a deadline to do her bidding...or pay the price.

He had to lose Maggie, or risk losing his job.

If she had enough votes—it could happen. He could lose his rightful position as head of Gale Incorporated. And all because...what? He hadn't picked a socialite to marry.

Because he made a mistake years ago, while he'd still been in college?

No. There had to be more to the story. Some reason that people besides his mother were prepared to kick him out. What was he *missing*?

"Everything okay over here?" Maggie asked, stopping in front of him. She cocked her head. "You look like you've seen a ghost."

"Not a ghost, exactly." He said, still staring at his mother. She stared right back at him, looking way too pleased with herself. "It's nothing."

Now wasn't the time to talk to her about this. He needed to think. To figure out his next move. If it came down to his job or her...he'd be forced to make a choice. But first he wanted to understand *why.*

"It obviously isn't nothing. You're upset." Maggie followed his line of sight. "What did she say to you?"

"Just the usual." He squared his shoulders and got his shit together. He was showing his mother that she'd gotten to him, and he couldn't afford to do that right now. Holding his hand out for hers, he asked, "Ready to go in?"

"Ah, there it is again," she said softly, without moving.

"There what is?"

"The beast." She bit the corner of her lip. "You don't have to talk to me if you don't want to, and I won't pressure you to tell me what she said, but it's okay to be upset. You can let me see it. Let me in."

His heart twisted, and he stepped closer to her. Smoothing her hair out of her face, he shook his head. "You said you couldn't read me."

"I guess I'm a little better at it." She rested her hands on his chest and stared up at him, her gray eyes matching the stormy sky above them. "Tell me the truth. Are you okay?"

"Yeah." He covered her hands with his and squeezed.

"I'll be fine."

"Still want to go in?"

He glanced over her head. His mother watched them closely, her shrewd stare not wavering in the slightest. She was even better than *he* was at hiding his emotions. If he left now, she'd see that she'd rattled him. He refused to give her that satisfaction.

"Yes. Let's go see the show. I've heard it's excellent."

She nodded once, not pressuring for more. As they headed for the doors, she asked, "Want me to go say 'whore' to her, so you can watch her faint from the vulgar language from her son's even more vulgar fiancée?"

He blinked down at her. The mental image of Andrew flailing at his mother's side, fanning her cheeks like a good little son, and everyone else running around like chickens with their heads chopped off, played out in his mind. "I—" He chuckled and then broke into laughter fully, cutting off midsentence. And there was no stopping it once it started.

When he tried, he only laughed *harder*.

Jesus, what was *wrong* with him?

When the ostentatious woman in front of him shot him an incredulous look, he clutched his stomach and kept going even though it hurt, and he couldn't stop. Nothing short of a punch to the face would make him, and even then, he probably wouldn't quit.

By the time he'd regained control, Maggie had joined him, her musical laughter mixing with his. His mother no longer looked quite so unaffected. She seemed *pissed*.

"Darling," he said, swiping his hands across his face. "You're killing me."

She smiled, her face lighting up. "It worked."

"What worked?"

"I made you laugh." She blew her bangs out of her face with a short puff of breath. "That's all I wanted."

"*You.*" He yanked her into his arms and pulled her into his arms. She gasped, resting her hands on his chest. "You're amazing. You know that, right?"

She shrugged and scrunched her nose up adorably. "I may have heard that a few times last night…"

"And you'll hear it again." He kissed her jaw. "And again." Her nose this time. "And again." He kissed her fully on the lips, and she clung to him.

By the time he pulled back, they were both out of breath.

She smiled up at him. This. Right here. This was what he wanted. And come what may, he'd fight to keep her and his job, too. He didn't want to lose her yet.

Hell, that wasn't true. He didn't want to lose her period. *Ever.* So whatever it took, no matter the cost—well, he guessed he was more like his mother than either one of them suspected.

He *would* win.

Chapter Fourteen

The second they entered Benjamin's apartment, he pulled Maggie into his arms and kissed her. He'd already excused William and sent him off, so they were finally alone. After watching the musical with him, her recent choices made perfect sense. All throughout the show, the words the characters sang had echoed pretty much every feeling and conversation *they'd* had about taking chances on one another, and not being afraid to leap blindly into something that could possibly be *every*thing.

Toward the end, during an emotional song about learning to live without the one you loved, he had glanced over at her, seen the tears streaming down her face, and caught her hand in his. And he hadn't let go of her for the rest of the musical. It was as if that entire score had been written for her, to teach her a lesson.

And she'd listened.

God, had she listened.

She had a feeling he had, too. He was oddly silent on the way home, as well as throughout dinner at The Monkey Bar, and now he kissed her with an abandon that was unparalleled. As if she was about to slip out of his hands. She felt it, too.

The desperation.

It was real, tangible, and as unavoidable as it was unwanted.

He pressed her back against the door of his apartment, slid his hand up her dress and skimmed his fingers between her thighs. His knuckles brushed against her core, and she groaned, her stomach twisting into a tight knot at his barely-there caress. She undid the buttons of his shirt with shaking fingers, as he cupped her, pressing his palm against her.

The second she had the last button undone; she shoved his jacket and shirt off in one swoop. They hit the floor, and he stepped closer, towering over her as he trapped her between the door and his chest. He tasted like wine and smelled like woodsy cologne. And felt like paradise.

She dragged her hands over his crisp chest hair and hard muscles. His tongue dueled with hers, and the unyielding urgency she felt inside engulfed her. He seemed to sense her need, because he picked her up. She wrapped her legs around his waist and her arms around his neck.

When he rubbed his hard length against her, she almost came. He groaned and undid his pants, not breaking off the kiss even for a second even as they hit the floor.

Twisting her head away, she gulped in a deep breath. He didn't waste any time putting his mouth to use elsewhere. He bit down on her shoulder, and sucked on it gently. "Benjamin. Yes. Now. *Please*."

He grunted and shoved her panties aside with two fingers. He ran them along her slit, slowly, torturously. "All I've been able to think about all damn day was getting you home, lifting this dress, and fucking you so hard you wouldn't be able to walk straight for the rest of the night. I need you, darling. I need you *now*."

Slipping his hands under her butt, he tilted her hips forward and drove into her with one thrust. She screamed and let loose a few curses.

He froze. "Shit, are you—?"

"I'm fine, and I'm on the pill. Have been for years." She smacked his arm. It was so hard it hurt her knuckles, but she was past caring about that. "Don't you dare stop. Do it again. *Harder.*"

Letting out a sexy chuckle, he buried his face in her neck and thrust inside her again. "How about that? Hard, fast, rough?"

"*Yes.*" She dug her nails in so deep they drew blood, but he didn't seem to care. Instead, he moved his hips even faster. And she—exploded. "*Benjamin.*"

He moved inside her relentlessly, not giving her time to catch her breath or come down from the orgasm he'd already given her. She lost track of how many times she hit him, or cried out, or came. All that mattered, and all she was aware of, was that she needed this man in her life more than she cared to admit.

More than she would've ever thought possible.

Pulling out of her, he set her on her feet and spun her so she faced the door. She flattened her palms on the cool steel, gasping as he ran his hands down the curve of her hip, and across her upper thigh. He grabbed it, his fingers brushing against her core.

"So damn pretty." Seizing her butt, he tilted her hips backward and kicked her legs apart. "So fucking mine."

She swallowed a moan. "Yes, I'm yours. And *you're* mine."

Fisting her hair, he pressed against her, his front glued to every inch of her back. His other hand splayed across her bare stomach, holding her exactly where he wanted her. "Damn right I am. Don't you ever doubt that. I'm all yours—happily and willingly."

His tender words were at odds with his dominant hold on her, but somehow that only made it all the more intimate. His fingers curled over the front of her core, pressing against her clit as he thrust them inside her. She bit her lip to hold back her moan. "Me too. I swear it."

The second the words came out of her mouth, she was flat against he door and he slammed inside of her again. She screamed, and the pleasure of the new angle blinded her momentarily. She scrambled for something to hold on to, but couldn't find anything. As if he sensed her need, he wrapped her in his embrace, one fist still in her hair, and thrust into her again.

Tension spiraled inside her, building higher and higher, until she was sure it would tear her in half. "I'm gonna...I..."

"Me too. Fuck, me too."

His uneven breath grew faster, more frantic, and so did his hips. The faster he moved, the higher she went, until she came *again*. And this time, when the world exploded around her, he was with her the whole way. He stiffened behind her, a guttural groan escaping him. "*Maggie,*" he said, long and low, drawn out like a sigh.

She dropped her head against the door, struggling to recover her balance when all she wanted to do was collapse into bed with him and never move again.

He broke the silence first. "I'm serious about what I said earlier."

"Which part?" she asked, peeking over her shoulder at him. She couldn't see his face, because it was buried in her neck. "You'll have to be more specific."

"I have no doubts." His hold on her hair loosened, and he dropped a kiss on her bare back. "You make me...*happy*. I didn't think I knew what that was, or if it was even a real thing, until you. But now I do, and I don't want to let go of it.

I don't want to let go of you."

Her heart fluttered in her chest. There he went again, trying to steal it. If she wasn't careful, she'd let him. "You make me happy, too. And in case you haven't noticed, I'm still holding onto your hand with both of mine. I don't want to let go either."

Without another word, he swept her into his arms. It wasn't until he held her close that she realized she hadn't even taken her purse off her shoulder. All of that insanely amazing sex had taken place without her removing an article of clothing. A giggle bubbled out of her.

Though he kept walking, he frowned down at her. "What's so funny?"

"I'm still wearing my purse." She held it up. "I didn't even take off my purse."

His lips twitched, and she burst into laughter. Shaking his head, he kicked his bedroom door open and laid her on his bed, a huge smile on his face. "The things you find funny…"

That only made her laugh even harder.

By the time she had herself under control, he'd put on a pair of sweats and walked into his closet. "I got you something. Don't be mad."

She swiped her hands across her wet cheeks and watched him, her heart picking up speed. "What did you do?"

"I saw this, and I couldn't help but think it would be perfect for the party at the Met on the twenty-third." He came out carrying a big pink box. "You usually pick your outfits, and I know you don't like me spending money on you, but I couldn't resist this one."

She reached out and took the box, her arms feeling weak and shaky. He bought her a dress? How very…prince-like of him. "Is it black?"

"No." He snorted. "Never."

Smiling, she played with the pink bow for a second before

undoing the knot. The second she lifted the lid off the box, she gasped. The most beautiful midnight blue dress she'd ever seen stared back at her. It was satin, and had intricate beading that looked like it was straight off an A-lister's back on the red carpet. "Oh my God. It's beautiful."

"I couldn't resist." He sat beside her, bending a knee and settling on his foot. He touched the dress, tracing one of the threads that led to the beads. "The blue matches those flecks that show up in your eyes when you smile. And since I plan on making you smile a lot that night, it seemed like it was made for you."

"It's perfect," she whispered, tears burning her eyes. "You're perfect. I love it. Thank you."

He curled his hand behind her neck, and kissed her. When he pulled back, his blue eyes were warmer than ever before. "You're the perfect one. Not me. I'm just me."

She wasn't sure what to say to that, so she kissed him instead.

And she didn't want to stop.

By the time they came up for air, they were both undressed and breathing heavily, and the dress had fallen to the floor. Yawning, Benjamin pulled the covers over them and settled in. She rolled onto her side, facing him, and folded her hands under her cheek. "I—" The ring of her phone cut her off. "Who could that be?"

He raised a brow. "I have no idea, since it's not my phone. Answer it, we'll find out."

"It's probably just—" Digging in her purse, she pulled out her cell and frowned down at the screen. "Oh. It's my parents. They never call this late. Could you give me a second?"

Benjamin sat up. "Sure. I'll go grab us a couple bottles of water."

"Thanks." She watched him go, waiting till he crossed the threshold and turned the corner. Then, and only then, she answered the phone. "What's wrong, Mom?"

"Nothing's wrong." She paused. "But Lou called a few minutes ago. We got word from the bank, and we're going to find out tomorrow at nine a.m. if we got the grant that could keep us running."

She held the phone tight, offering a silent prayer that they would get it. If they didn't, her parents would lose the farm, and everything they worked so hard to build all these years. "Did Lou give you any indication of the verdict when he called?"

"No, he said he wasn't told yet. He just heard the answer was waiting for him on his desk." She let out a small sigh. "I don't have a good feeling about this."

"Don't think like that. You have to think positively." Maggie flopped back on the bed and stared up at the fan above Benjamin's bed. Unlike hers back home, his did *not* need to be dusted. It was impeccably clean. His sheets were soft and satiny, and everything looked...*rich*. Different. It didn't feel like home. "If you believe it can be saved, it will. You taught me that."

Her mom laughed. "I did, didn't I?"

"Yes." She peeked at the door, but there was no sign of Benjamin. "The farm won't be shut down. I swear I'll do everything I can to make sure it stays open, before we have to resort to something drastic and final."

"That's not your job, dear," her mom said, her voice sad. "It's mine. And this *is* our last resort. We've exhausted every avenue we could. If we don't get a loan or a grant...it's over."

She rubbed her forehead, worry taking over despite her words to her mother. All her life, her father had worked hard to keep *his* father's farm going...and for what? To lose it now? *No*. That couldn't be how this ended. "I refuse to accept that. There has to be a way to get the money. There just has to." Footsteps came down the hallway, and Maggie cleared her throat. "Don't lose faith."

"I won't," her mom said.

Benjamin hovered in the doorway, and she motioned him inside, sitting up and folding her knees in front of her. She hadn't wanted him to hear this conversation, but it was pretty much over now. He wouldn't understand the struggle her parents faced, and would probably offer to throw money at the problem to fix it, and as much as that might help, she refused to be yet another hand held out for him to fill. "I have to go now. I'm not at home."

He walked in, two bottles of water in his hand, and sat down on his side of the bed. Slowly, he rubbed her back in large, sweeping circles.

"Are you at that guy's house?" Her mother asked. "The one you told me about?"

Maggie flinched, side-eyeing him. He smiled back. "Yes."

"Is he there now?"

"Yes…"

Her mom whispered. "Can he hear me?"

"Yes," she whispered back. "He probably can."

His hand froze on her. Leaning in, he whispered, "Why are we all whispering? Is someone listening to us?"

A laugh escaped Maggie, and she covered her mouth. "Okay, I have to go now. Love you, Mom. And…don't worry. It'll all be fine. You'll see."

He resumed rubbing her back as she hung up. When she finished, she tossed her phone aside and hugged her knees. He sat up, scooting behind her, and rested his chin on her shoulder. "You told your parents about me?"

"Yeah." She leaned over to peer at him. "Is that a bad thing?"

"No." He resumed rubbing. "I told my mom about us, too."

She rolled her eyes. "No, really?"

"Really." Chuckling, he kissed her neck. "Is everything okay, though? You sounded upset."

"It's fine." She shrugged. "I'm fine."

"Okay..."

Silence descended, and she couldn't think of anything to say to fill it. So she said nothing, just let herself enjoy the sensation of his hand moving over her back, slow and steady. "Remember when I told you my father died of a heart attack, and I was too busy partying to bother to show up in time?"

She lifted her lids, blinking slowly, her heart wrenching. This time, his voice was laced with pain, and his pain physically *hurt* her, because he was finally letting her in. He blamed himself, and his mother blamed him, too, which made her long to pull him into her arms, hug him, and promise him that it would all be okay. "Yeah?"

His hand paused. "When I finally listened to my voicemail and found out what happened, I rushed to the hospital, breaking all kinds of traffic laws, but he had died ten minutes before I got there. My mother...she wouldn't even let me see him before they took him away. I didn't fight it, because I felt like I deserved every ounce of shit I got from her. I've spent the last few years trying to become a man he would have been proud of. Trying to model myself after him."

She rolled over and raised up on an elbow. The lights were out, but the moonlight and the lights of the city illuminated the room enough for her to see him, and he looked...guilty. Ashamed. Torn. And she wanted to fix him.

"You don't have to change who you are, Benjamin. I bet if your father were here—wait, scratch that. He is here. And he's watching. I'm positive he's pretty freaking proud of what you've accomplished."

He smoothed her hair back. "I'm not so sure. The man you see at the office, the one I was before you came into my life? That's the me I was trying to be. The me I was trying to become. But with you…I can't do it. I can't be pragmatic, focused, and completely dedicated to my work. You make me too happy."

He sounded awfully unhappy about being happy. "Is that a bad thing, or good?"

"I haven't figured that out yet." He lay down and held his arms out for her. "Will you stay the night with me, darling? I don't want to lose you."

She curled up in his arms. "There's nowhere else I'd rather be."

As his arms closed around her, she took a deep breath and closed her eyes, breathing his scent in. There was no telling what tomorrow would bring, but with Benjamin's arms around her, the apartment didn't feel so foreign anymore.

It felt like…*home.*

Chapter Fifteen

The next afternoon, Benjamin sat behind his desk, rubbed his forehead, and cursed his sleepless night. Even though he'd held Maggie in his arms, which should have soothed him, he'd been unable to relax enough to actually drift off. And man, he was paying for it now. He'd spent the day in a council meeting, pouring over financials and reports.

At first, he'd been so sure he would find something—*anything*—that would explain his mother's behavior, as well as her insistence that he marry for money. Like they were impoverished and needed funds. Or maybe the company was going under.

But that wasn't the case.

Since he joined the company, the profits were up nearly two hundred percent. He didn't understand why she was so unhappy with him, or what drove her to try to kick him out of his seat. The board seemed as confused about the turn of events as he was.

The company was safe. The board was happy.

All evidence pointed to his mother being a rich, heartless

snob. But he couldn't believe that was the *only* reason. There had to be something else.

Tossing the papers down with a frustrated sigh, he leaned back in his chair and covered his face. His company was perfectly fine—which should make him happy. It did, but it pissed him off at the same time. On top of his mother's stressful deadline hanging over his head like a fucking anvil, Maggie had been acting strange.

Ever since her parents had called, she'd been quiet. Reserved. Upset, even. He'd heard her mention money on the phone, and coming up with a way to find some, but he hadn't pried because she clearly wasn't in the mood to talk about it. That was killing him, too.

Especially after *he* opened up to *her* like that.

The door to his office swung in, and he didn't bother to take his hands off his face. The only person who would walk in without knocking was Maggie. "What's up?"

"That's no way to greet your mother."

Oh, just fucking great. He lowered his hands and sat up straight, standing unsteadily. "Mother. What a pleasant surprise."

"I bet it is." She shut the door behind her and walked up to his desk. Before he could so much as come around to dutifully kiss her forehead, she tossed down a thick folder. "This is what you're looking for. You won't find it in those reports, or hear about it in a board meeting with a bunch of clueless investors."

He glanced down at the pile. "Won't find what?"

"The evidence that this company needs a merger with Reginald to keep running. I've kept it hidden from you because I didn't want you find out how your father ran us into the ground, but I should have told you years ago." She smoothed her hair. "It's why I kept pushing you to marry Elizabeth. If you do, Reginald will save us."

"How did you…?" He rested his hand on his hard thigh, his heart thumping so fast and hard it physically hurt as he opened the folder and glanced at the papers. "Wait. What?"

"When you called a board meeting, I was informed. They also told me you went over financials extensively, so it was clear what you were seeking." With a manicured finger, she tapped the paper he'd flipped over. "These are the real reports. The ones no one but the two of us can *ever* see."

He stared down at his desk blindly, his heart thumping a loud staccato in his head. "But how would no one else find out about it? All the shareholders, and board members… That doesn't make any sense. They would have to know."

"No, they don't. Because I've kept it from them." She collapsed in the chair in front of this desk. For the first time in his life, she looked *defeated*. Probably because what she'd done was illegal, and they both knew it. "I've hidden the truth from everyone. I only just told Andrew this past weekend."

He shook his head. "But…*how*?"

"How did I keep it a secret? Or how did it all fall apart in the first place?"

He glanced at the papers in front of him, turning another paper over. Sure enough, a bunch of dire looking numbers stared back at him, and he tossed it back down angrily. "Both."

"I've always been good at hiding what I want to hide, once I put my mind to it. At putting on a show. A good face." She rubbed her forehead. "As for the other question, we lost everything through a series of bad decisions made by your father that led to financial ruin. We're doomed, Benjamin, and need an influx of money if we're going to survive."

His heart thudded in his ears, and he tugged on his tie because, Jesus Christ, it was trying to fucking strangle him. "I…see."

"Do you?" His mother leaned forward, a penetrating

stare latched on to him like a hawk. "Reginald agreed to bail out the company if you marry Elizabeth. We need her money. Gale Incorporated needs it, or it'll die. And your father's memory, with it."

A heavy weight fell to the pit of his stomach. It felt a hell of a lot like responsibility laced with a healthy dose of dread. It also felt like the death of any hope of happiness with Maggie. "Why didn't you tell me sooner? I could have tried to do something."

She lifted a dainty shoulder. "I didn't think it would come to this. I thought you would do your duty and marry Elizabeth, as you should have all along. But you went and picked that woman, and you've forced my hand. Don't worry. Your 'fiancée' will bolt as soon as she discovers you're poor. I have no doubt of that. Gold diggers like her always flee at the slightest scent of poverty."

"She's not—" He stiffened, rage pumping through his veins instead of blood. For the first time, he let himself feel anger toward his mother. And it was because of Maggie that he could do this—the same Maggie he was now going to lose. "You know what? Get the hell out of my office."

"I understand that you're upset, but that's no way to talk to your mother." She stood, smoothing her flawless business skirt. "I'll go. But Elizabeth is stopping by in three hours. I told her you'll be asking her to marry you, and I expect you to follow through."

Rage blinded him even more, and he pushed to his feet, taking a step toward her. "How *dare* you tell her such a thing?"

"I dare because I have faith you'll do the right thing, for once in your life." She eyed him, her lip curled in disgust. "I raised you to do it. I expect it. So does your father. Or are you going to let him down *again*?"

Without waiting for an answer, she swept out of his office,

shutting the door behind her. He watched her through the window that led out into the main office area—his attention on one person in particular.

Maggie sat at her desk, holding her head, looking as if she was about to cry. His mother stopped to speak to her, and she tensed.

Swallowing hard, he closed the blinds and ignored the gut instinct to go out there and make sure she was all right. Instead, he sat at his desk and picked up the papers his mother had dropped on his desk. Unfortunately, he found exactly what he'd been looking for all day long. He found the reason why his mother wanted him to marry up.

And there was no escaping the undeniable truth. If he wanted to save his father's company, he'd have to do the unthinkable. He'd have to marry Elizabeth and be miserable for the rest of his goddamn life.

He closed his eyes, Maggie's laugh ringing through his head. It only made him feel even more depressed, because he was about to lose that. Lose her. Everything was about to slip out of his hands, because he had to save his father's company.

The door opened again, but stopped halfway.

Someone knocked.

He scowled at it, and whoever dared to interrupt him. "Who is it?"

"It's me." Maggie peeked her head in, and her fresh-faced beauty was like a punch in the throat. "Do you have a second?"

Everything he'd wanted and couldn't have, stared him right in the face. *Mocked* him. He'd been so damn sure they could make things work, and now he had to let her go. That hurt a hell of a lot more than it should have, which only pissed him off more.

"I'm busy," he said through clenched teeth. "Make it quick."

She shut the door behind her but didn't come inside the office more than necessary. She clutched the knob, shifting on her feet. "Are you okay?"

"No," he bit out. "I'm not fucking okay. Now isn't a good time."

She blinked, clearly taken aback at him snapping her head off. "Oh. Sorry."

When she didn't speak any more, he gestured for her to get on with it. He was being an ass, but he couldn't seem to stop. He was going to lose her because of something his father did—and that pissed him the hell off. It might not be her fault, but right now, it felt like it was. "Well? What did you want?"

She hesitated, and he wanted to scream at her to get the hell out before he said or did something he'd regret, but he didn't make a sound. He just sat there like a fucking fool. "I have to...I mean...I had a question. My parents got bad news today, and...well, uh, I—"

Something inside of him exploded, and there was no stopping the flow of words once they came. He'd just found out he was all but trapped in an arranged marriage he didn't want, and she couldn't get a damn sentence out? "Jesus Christ. Spit it the fuck out. I don't have all damn day to sit here while you get up the nerve to speak."

Her jaw dropped. "What's your problem? Forget it. I don't want your help anymore."

"Great. Just fucking great."

"Screw you." Turning her back on him, she fumbled with the doorknob, but her hands trembled too badly to turn it. "Come *on,* you stupid *door.*"

He shoved his chair back and stalked across the room to her. She finally managed to get it open, but he thumped a hand on the wood, shutting it with a loud *bang.* "What. Did. You. Want?"

She spun, her back against the door. "N-Nothing. Forget it."

"Maggie." He gritted his teeth together, trying to get a hold on his temper. It wasn't her fault his world was falling apart. She didn't do anything wrong, and he shouldn't be snarling in her face like the beast he was. "Just tell me."

"I—I'm leaving."

A knife of pain sliced through his chest. Out of all the things he expected her to say, this was pretty much at the bottom of the list. "Where are you going?"

"Home. I have to—" She cut herself off, pressing her lips together. "I mean, I quit. I can't be your researcher, or your fiancée, or…your anything."

What the *hell* was going on today?

He'd been trying to find a way to tell her the same thing, that he couldn't be her anything, but now that he faced it, he couldn't lose her. "What happened? What's changed?"

"Everything's changed. I—I have to go."

"Tell me why, damn it." He backed her against the door even more, refusing to budge. Not till he had some sort of answer. "Why are you leaving me?"

"Stop *yelling* at me," she snapped, her face pale. "Let me go. I want to go."

Funny. He hadn't even realized he'd raised his voice.

"Damn it. I—I need you. Need *this*. You can't just—" *Walk away from me.* "I'm sorry I yelled. Please, just—just—" *Forgive me.*

Unable to put his words into actual words, he slammed his mouth down on hers, trapping her between the door and his chest. He couldn't just throw her away and act as if she didn't matter. Marry someone else and forget all about her. He couldn't *do* it.

There had to be another way. What they had, it was special. What they had…it was…it was…*love*. That's what the wrenching, stabbing pain in his chest was. He *loved* her, and he didn't want to lose her. Not when she'd only just shown him how to live.

She shoved his shoulders and twisted herself free. "I said *let me go*."

He stumbled back, shock punching him in the gut. "Jesus. What's—?"

"I have to go home to South Dakota." She balled her hands and lifted her chin. "I just wanted to tell you that I'm leaving. I have to go pack, or I'll miss my flight. It's over. I can't be your fiancée anymore."

It was happening. She was leaving him. And she hadn't even thought twice about it. Or him. While he'd been playing the part of a lovesick fool, she'd been busily planning her departure. Just like that, she'd washed her hands of him. "Wow."

She tugged on a piece of hair. "I just—you can't help me out of this. You can't—it's not something your money—"

He stiffened. "Money? What the hell does money have to do with—?" He broke off, the pieces of the puzzle forming into one giant ugly-ass picture. His mother had been right all along. He was broke, and she was jumping ship. That didn't make any sense...and yet, it did. It really fucking did. "My mother already told you, didn't she?"

She blinked. "Wait, what? I—"

"Never mind, I don't give a damn what the hell you have to say at this point." He swept his hand, virtually shooing her away like an unwanted pest. "Get the fuck out of here. Don't let the door hit you on the ass on the way out."

"*Benjamin*." Her face paled. "I didn't mean to hurt you," she said softly. "But I have to—"

"—Go. Yeah. I got that loud and clear, Ms. Donovan." He crossed his arms. "So, go, then. No one's stopping you, least of all me. You want out? You're out."

She grabbed the doorknob, but didn't turn it. Mumbling, she faced him again. "You're angry with me. Let me explain—"

Angry? That didn't even begin to cover what he was feeling.

Betrayed. Gutted. Hurt. *Alone*. Those words all applied to how he felt.

"I'm not angry. I'm just waiting for you to get the hell out."

Still, she hesitated. "Look, I'm sorry I didn't have the opportunity to give the proper two weeks' notice," she said, her voice low and hesitant. "I hope that won't affect any references I might need from the company. And I'm sorry if I let you down."

He was rocking from the pain of her leaving him, just as his mother predicted, because he'd lost his money, and she was worried about her *references*? Well, fuck that. And fuck her. This is what happened when you let someone in. They hurt you. She'd been right. Trust was a weapon, and she stabbed him in the back without a second thought. "I don't give a damn about any of that. If you're going, go. I don't care."

She nodded, her lower lip trembling. She bit down on it hard.

He walked back to his desk, not even looking back at her as she left. There was no point. It was over, and she didn't give a damn. So neither would he. The door shut behind her, and he bent over his desk, gripping the edge so tightly it was amazing he didn't break the wood. He wished he had, because damn it all to hell, he wanted to break shit.

Lots of it.

Shoving the papers off his desk, he picked up the hockey puck because it reminded him of her, and chucked that across the room, too. It bounced off the wall and fell to the floor without breaking anything. He couldn't even do that right. *"Son of a fucking bitch."*

The door opened again, and he growled. What the hell was this, Grand Central Station? Elizabeth poked her blonde head in, looking scared of him.

Good. She should be.

"Is this a bad time?"

Yes. "No."

She walked in and shut the door behind her, taking in the mess he'd made. "I gather your mother told you I'd be coming by."

"Yeah." He walked over to the scotch on the bar, opened the bottle, and raised it to his mouth. No point in even bothering with a glass. He'd need the whole bottle to get through this. "We're supposed to get married and live happily ever after now, because my mother says we have to. That sound about right?"

She played with the leather straps on her pink purse. "Well…yeah. Basically."

He put the bottle down hard, his muscles trembling with impotent rage. He didn't want this. He wanted Maggie…but she obviously didn't want him. She'd left without a sign of doubt or regret, and hadn't even told him *why*.

But that was okay, because he knew why she left. He was broke.

"You want to marry me," he said, glaring out the window.

She hesitated again. "Yes."

"Why?" He turned on her, and she jumped, as if she was afraid he might bite. And yet she wanted to fucking marry him. "Why the hell would you want to marry me? I'm apparently poor, as well as a jerk. We never really got along when we were dating, and the chemistry between us is pretty much nonexistent."

She crossed the room and stared up at him, her intent

clear. "That's not true." She clasped his suit jacket, holding on for dear life, and kissed him. He stiffened when her tongue touched his. She let out a soft moan and pressed more firmly against him, deepening the kiss, and he let her because he was desperate to feel something. Anything.

He felt *nothing*. Except sick.

Cursing inwardly, he ended the kiss, swiped a hand across his mouth, and downed more scotch. It was what he'd expected—she did nothing for him, and never would. The only person who'd been able to fill him with an undying need to touch and feel had left him. He was doomed to be the unfeeling beast they all thought he was.

"See?" she said, her chest rising and falling. She watched him like some sort of starved animal. "Electrifying."

Gripping the bottle tightly, he tossed back more. "I can't marry you."

"Yes, you can." She walked up behind him and rested her hands on his back. "And you will."

"No." He shook his head. "I'd eat you alive like the monster I am. You don't want to be married to a guy like me. I'll make you miserable, and you'll want to kill me, or yourself, or both of us. It *won't* work. Trust me."

"But I want to marry you." She ran her fingers over his shoulders. "I always have. I don't love you, and I don't want you to love me. I just want to unite our families. Build a legacy to hand down to our kids, and their kids, and so on."

He laughed, unable to believe he was hearing this and not telling her to go fuck herself, and even more unable to believe that Maggie had just *left* him. "I think you're crazy."

She watched him with so much greed, desire…and something else he couldn't quite name…it made him sick. "At least think about it? Don't dismiss it out of hand."

He'd just told her he'd make her life a living hell, and she was *okay* with that? Well, if that's what she wanted, and she was okay with hating him, then what the hell ever. It didn't matter anymore because the only woman he'd ever loved walked out of his life the second he lost his cash.

"Want a drink?" he asked, wiggling the bottle.

"With you?" She nodded and pressed against him. "Yes."

He poured a glass, handing it off. Saluting her, he said, "To a world without love and pain."

And then he took another shot.

Chapter Sixteen

After telling the cab driver to wait outside the office building, Maggie made her way back up to Benjamin's office. He'd been on edge before she'd even told him her news, and it had freaked her out. He'd been harsh. Angry. Different. Scary, even.

So she hadn't really felt like opening up to him and telling him about her parent's financial issues. But now that she'd had time to think rationally, maybe she should have been a little bit more open. If nothing else, she should have demanded he tell her what he'd meant when he mentioned his mother.

His mother had been in there with him. She'd obviously upset him, and then Maggie leaving without explaining why had probably put him over the edge. It didn't give him a reason to be such a jerk, but he didn't handle that kind of stress well. And had trouble with his emotions.

She needed to find out what had really gone on back in his office.

Give him a chance to explain.

Over the time they'd spent together, he had come to mean a lot to her, and she needed to tell him that her leaving had nothing to do with him. Her family was *actually* losing their farm. The one constant in her life was going away, and there was nothing she could do to stop it. She couldn't help them. But she had to go home and try anyway.

There was already an investor interested in purchasing the land for development, and her parents had been urged to accept. So they were. Already. Everything was happening so fast, and she needed to pack up her old room, say good-bye to her childhood home and look for a new one, and—

It hurt. It hurt *so* much.

But despite all that, he deserved an explanation on why she'd cut out on him like that. The elevator doors opened, and she stepped into the office, pressing her thumb against the back of the ring he had given her. She would have to take it off and return it. No matter what he'd said on that first date, she couldn't keep it.

It wouldn't be right.

Everyone else was gone, but he'd still be there working, like usual. She walked up to his door, reached out for the knob—and froze, because he wasn't alone.

Elizabeth, his ex, was with him.

An empty bottle of scotch lay on the table, tipped over on its side, and Benjamin sat in the same chair he had when they'd had their first "date." He'd taken his suit jacket off and loosened his collar, while Elizabeth paced in front of him, talking animatedly.

He watched her through hooded lids.

The other woman stopped in front of him and knelt between his legs, resting her greedy little hands on his thighs. He didn't move away. Elizabeth said a few more words, he nodded, and she rose on her knees, pressing her mouth to his.

"No." Pain pierced through Maggie, and she swallowed back a cry, pressing a hand over her mouth. He'd obviously moved on. "*No.*"

"Charming, isn't it?" someone said behind her. She *recognized* that voice. And hated it. "They found one another again."

Maggie stiffened. "Let me guess. You gave him a little push after I left?"

"That's what mothers do, isn't it?" Mrs. Gale asked, smirking. "Guide our children into making the right choices. We'll stop at nothing to ensure they reach their full potential, and I assure you, I'm more determined than most mothers."

She turned her back on whatever was going on inside Benjamin's office, refusing to look again. She'd seen enough. "I'm glad you got what you wanted, Helen. I just hope *he* does, too."

"Don't worry, he'll be just fine. He's missed her ever since she left him. He loved her," she added, pouring salt on the wounds she'd ripped into Maggie. "Always has, ever since they were children. You can't compete with something like that."

"I thought *he* left *her*," she said.

"Is that what he told you?" The older woman laughed. "And you believed him? Have you seen her?"

Maggie didn't say anything. She couldn't, because her heart was being shredded with each passing moment.

And it hurt even more than losing her childhood home had.

"Poor, naive child." She shook her head. "He probably wanted to save face, because he couldn't get over losing her. This whole charade with you was a ploy to get her attention, and it worked."

Maggie blinked rapidly. "I don't believe you."

"You don't have to believe me. You saw it with your own eyes." She waved a hand dismissively. "Run along now, child. Your job here is finished, and your parents will be needing you in this trying time."

Maggie stole one last look at him. The kiss had ended. He paced back and forth, talking. She couldn't see Elizabeth's face, but it looked like she lifted her hands and covered it. Maggie wanted to yank them off until she had nothing but bloody stumps left on the ends of her arms. But his mother was right.

He was obviously done with her, and her parents would be—

"Wait a second." She crossed her arms, understanding sinking in despite the pain wracking her. "How did you find out about my parents?"

"Oh. About that?" The other woman gave a gloating smile. "I'm the buyer."

She shook her head, reeling. "What? *Why?*"

"It got rid of you." Mrs. Gale shrugged. "And now you know that I could destroy your parents' last chance of getting a profit out of that tiny piece of dry, unworkable land." She snapped her fingers. "It would be that easy to ruin them. To ruin you."

She curled her hands into fists, dropping her arms at her sides, and fought the urge that screamed at her to scratch the woman's eyes out, one then the other. She was evil. Pure, unadulterated evil. "You wouldn't."

"Oh, but I *would*. And I'd enjoy it, too. It's what I'm best at, squashing little ants that threaten my plans." She pointed at the door. "So I suggest you leave before he sees you, and before I decide to step on you just for fun."

Tears blurred her vision. "Why are you doing this to me...to *us*?"

"Oh, honey. We've been in a battle since the second I found you under that table." She shrugged and stared over her shoulder. "And I refuse to do business with a woman like you for another second. Get out, or your parents lose everything."

She glowered at her. "You're a vile person. All you do is twist and turn things until you get what you want, and you treat your own son like a criminal. At some point, he's going to stop accepting your hatred as his punishment. At some point, he'll have enough, and you'll lose him, too."

Looking completely unaffected, she shrugged. "That might be true. But regardless, if you want my money to save your parents from living in destitution for the rest of their lives, run along quickly, and forget all about Benjamin Gale. He's not for you."

"You're wrong. He's not for you," Maggie snapped. "You don't deserve someone like him for a son. He's a good guy, you're just too much of a coldhearted bitch to appreciate it."

The witch checked her watch. "If you miss that flight, I'll retract my offer and spread word that the land isn't worth anything. No one else will buy it, and your parents will be penniless. And it'll be all your fault."

"I—" Maggie glanced at Benjamin again.

He had his hands on Elizabeth's shoulders and spoke quietly—completely oblivious to what his mother was doing to her just outside his door. Not that he cared. It was clear his mother had been telling the truth.

He'd gotten what he wanted—his ex.

And she had handed him to her on a gold platter.

Had Benjamin really done this? Had he used Maggie to get his ex back? Had he cared about her at all, or had it been an act? It didn't matter, really. Her heart had just been ripped out of her chest, and he was happy with the woman he'd apparently always loved. He didn't care about Maggie. He had what he wanted. He had Elizabeth.

Screw him.

They deserved each other.

Maggie stiffened, anger settling over her like a cloak, and walked away. As she passed her desk, she laid the ring he'd given her on it, right next to the credit card he insisted she take. She didn't need the reminder that she'd leaped off a cliff for him, and he hadn't caught her.

And she'd never forgive him for that.

Benjamin looked into Elizabeth's eyes, willing himself to feel something—*any*thing—for the woman quite literally begging him to marry her. But he got zilch, nada, zip. Instead, he found himself incredibly *bored*. And it only made him miss Maggie even more than he already did. What had she done to him?

Elizabeth stared up at him, all wide eyes and pouting lips. Her hands rested on his chest, and she rubbed him in a way that was probably supposed to arouse him, but was just annoying. "What are you saying?"

He tensed, unable to stand her hands moving over him for another second. He couldn't do this. He couldn't spend the rest of his life with this woman.

Jesus, he'd rather die.

"I'm saying that I can't marry you." He forcibly removed her hands from his body. "You need to leave. *Now*."

"But—"

He pointed to the door. "Leave. Now."

She gathered her purse to her chest, hugging it, and her lower lip trembled. Unlike Maggie, she did nothing to attempt to stop it. Maggie…

Was he too late? Had she already left?

"You're a real beast. You know that?" Elizabeth asked, sniffing.

"Yeah. I do." He picked up his phone and swiped his finger across it. "I'm surprised it took you so long to notice, though."

She swept off without another word.

He dialed Maggie's number and prayed like hell that he wasn't too late. That she hadn't gotten on the plane yet.

She couldn't leave him. He couldn't let her. He *loved* her.

As the phone rang, he stared at a paper on the floor, squinting at the tiny print. The dates…they were off. This was dated a little over six years ago, right before his father had passed away. He blinked, just in case the booze was fucking with his head.

It wasn't. These were *old* figures.

"What the hell?" he muttered, bending down and picking it up.

"That was uncalled for," his mother said, making him jump and curse under his breath. The paper floated back to the floor. He let it. "She's always been a nice girl. Far too nice for a spoiled brat such as yourself."

He turned to his mother, the phone still held to his ear. "Jesus Christ. How long have you been standing there watching me?"

"*Benjamin.*" She scowled at him. "Language."

Voicemail picked up, so he turned his back on his mother.

"*Hey, it's Maggie. I'm not available at the moment, so leave a message. Bye.*"

He swallowed hard, her voice sending a shaft of agony rushing through his veins. "It's me. Call me back. We need to talk." He paused, glanced at his mother, and added, "I'm sorry. Please. Call me." He hung up and slid his phone across the desk.

"She's gone." His mother crossed her arms. "I watched her go."

He froze, his heart pounding full speed ahead. "When did you see her?"

"When you were busy kissing Elizabeth. She saw that, too." She sat down on the chair by the door—the one he hadn't sat in because it was Maggie's, and it hadn't felt right. "Don't worry, though. She wasn't upset. The money she made off of you was well worth it."

He pressed a hand to his chest, as if it would ease the empty ache within, and picked the paper up again. Staring down at the date, he crumpled it into a ball, seething with the knowledge that he'd been had. These numbers were out of date, and he'd fallen for the oldest trick in the book. "What did you do?"

"Nothing. I simply informed her you wouldn't be able to buy her farm, like she'd hoped. It's why she roped you in. Her parents finally lost the valiant battle to keep their useless, insignificant business afloat. She was going to beg you to buy it and save her." She rested an arm on the table next to her and traced an invisible pattern. "So I told her that wouldn't happen, but that I'd buy it if she left. So I did. And she did."

He shook his head slowly, cursing the drink that fogged up his brain. "You bought her off, and she *took* it?"

"She did." She smiled and pulled something out of her purse. "Here's the paperwork, in case you don't believe me."

"But—" He took the documents and sure enough, it was paperwork to buy a large lot of land in South Dakota. And the dates were accurate on *these* papers. "It was all a lie. The money...it's there. It's all there."

She sighed. "Figured that out, did you? I'm not surprised. You always were a bright boy, when you chose to apply yourself. You simply chose not to."

"Yeah. I did." Benjamin blinked. "*Why did you do this?*"

"She had to think you were poor and couldn't help her. And you had to believe you were poor, too, or she wouldn't buy it, and you wouldn't have let her go. You gave me the idea when you started poking around in the financials. So, the credit truly goes to you. I dug out those old papers, handed them off, and the rest just fell into place. It was perfect, really." Her smile widened. "You're not a pauper after all. You don't need to marry Elizabeth—though I still wish you would—and that backwoods gold digger is out of our lives once and for all. I won."

Rage—*so much fucking rage*—blinded him. And he let it.

Lifting a trembling hand, he pointed to the door. "Get out."

"All right. I have dinner plans anyway." His mother stood, staring him down. "Be angry all you want, but you'll thank me later, when you meet a proper woman and realize I saved you from the biggest mistake of your life."

No, she hadn't, because he didn't believe a word she said. Maggie wouldn't have taken a bribe. "What was *your* biggest mistake? Having me?"

"Close enough." His mother hesitated. "Pretending you were mine."

"What?" he asked, the world ceasing to exist around him. She'd just said— "Are you saying I'm not your son?"

"Of course you're not. Your father slept with his secretary a year after we got married, and got her pregnant." His mother spat it out, anger radiating off her in waves. "Not wanting to face the shame, I helped him cover it up—and buy her off. I went on a European tour, and came back with a baby. With *you*. And I've hated you ever since."

His heart pounded loudly, echoing in his head. "I'm not your son?"

"You're not."

Suddenly, it all made sense.

Her hatred. Her preference for Andrew. The way she treated him. It all fell into place, and instead of being upset she wasn't his real mother, he felt...

Free. Absolutely, one hundred percent, *free*.

"Where's my real mother?"

"Dead." She hugged herself. "Has been since you were five."

He rubbed his jaw and nodded. "Thank you."

"Wh—?" She blinked at him, clearly taken aback. "For what?"

"The truth. I feel a lot better about you hating me now,

and even understand why." He inclined his head toward the door. "Now, if you'll excuse me?"

She started for the exit. "I didn't tell you to make you feel better," she snapped.

Refusing to give her the satisfaction of an answer, he gritted his teeth until she left. Once she did, he picked up the phone, and dialed Maggie's number again. She still didn't answer. He hung up and kicked his desk. "*Son of a bitch*."

He scowled out into the empty office, toward her desk—until he saw the glinting item on top of it. Storming out of his office, he headed straight for the gleaming object.

The ring. She'd left him the ring.

A gold digger wouldn't do that.

As he knew all along, his mother's story was just that. An elaborate story meant to make him despise Maggie. She wasn't who his mother said she was. She hadn't betrayed him. She might have been trying to save her parents' farm, but she hadn't pretended she cared about him just to get her hands on his money.

He couldn't believe that. Wouldn't.

And he never should have let her go.

Dialing again, he waited for voicemail to pick up. It did. Once her message ended, the phone beeped, and he pinched the bridge of his nose. "I don't believe you took the money as a bribe, so you have to tell me I'm right. Call me back and tell me you didn't use me to save your farm. *Tell me*."

Met with silence—obviously—he hung up and left the office.

One way or another, he'd find a way to fix this. To make it up to her that he'd believed the worst of her, when she'd done nothing but show him the best.

She deserved better, and he'd be the one to give it to her.

Chapter Seventeen

A week and a half later, on December Twenty-third, Maggie stood outside in the cool sunlight, wearing jeans and a plaid shirt and feeling anything but *merry*. They'd been busily cleaning out the house ever since she'd arrived, brokenhearted after realizing that Benjamin hadn't cared about her, and never would. He'd used her to get his fiancée back, and she'd fallen for every single word he'd said.

Like the stupid, naive idiot she was. Well, not anymore. She was done. With New York City. And him. Just...*done*. She didn't belong in that city, or his world.

Since she wasn't going back to New York, she would never have to see him or his deep blue eyes ever again. And she couldn't be happier about that. Ecstatic. Thrilled. Happy as a pig in mud, or a horse with a fresh pile of straw.

Rolling her eyes, she tossed the garbage in the can.

Even *she* didn't believe herself.

She was miserable, flat out miserable, and she missed him more than she'd have ever thought possible. He'd left a hole in her soul that she was beginning to suspect would never be filled, and he didn't even know how much he broke her heart.

And *that* hurt, too.

But for the sake of her parents, she'd been doing her best to act as if there was nowhere she'd rather be than back home, because if she didn't, they would feel bad. They'd been through enough already.

Mrs. Gale, for her part, had held to the bargain...so far.

She'd offered an extremely generous buying price, and her parents had accepted. They were now looking for a new home to buy with the profits, and had also started a job search. Everything was working out the best that it possibly could, and everyone was happy, all things considered.

Everyone except Maggie.

Benjamin kept calling and leaving voicemails on her cell, but she hadn't listened to any of them. If he left long messages thanking her for giving him what he'd always wanted...she'd throw up all over herself. It wasn't that she wasn't happy for him. She was. But she would rather die than listen to him tell her how happy he was.

Especially when she *so* wasn't.

The farm truck flew up the driveway and skidded to a stop. Maggie squinted and held a hand over her brows, shielding her vision from the sun. "What the—?"

"Maggie!" Her mom hopped out like the freaking Energizer bunny on crack, brandishing a piece of paper over her head like some kind of award. "Look! Come look!"

She dusted off her hands and bolted to her mother's side, her heart leaping. If Helen had backed out last minute... "What? What is it?"

"We've been awarded a grant. Some big league heavy hitter in New York paid off our debt and is letting us keep the farm." She waved the paper again. "Some sort of new forgiveness program for little food-producing farms like ours. Can you *believe* it?"

No. She couldn't believe it.

Not at *all*.

She snatched the letter out of her hand, skimming over it. Sure enough, she saw exactly what she expected to see. Benjamin Gale's name on the letter. But...why would he do that? He'd done the very thing she'd asked him not to do. He paid her off.

After breaking her heart.

The anger and hurt rose up, choking her, but she forced a smile for her mother's benefit, because now that he'd done it, there was no going back. Her parents got to keep the farm, which was great, but it had come from the man who'd ruined her...which was not so freaking great. "Wow. Go tell Dad. He'll be so happy."

"I know." Her mother hugged her, and ran off for the house. "Glen!"

She let the smile fade as soon as her mom went inside. How dare he pay off her debt, as if that made up for all the lies he'd told her? All the pain he'd caused?

It didn't.

And she would tell him as much.

She took her phone out of her pocket at the same time as an unfamiliar SUV pulled up the driveway. She watched, dread settling in the pit of her stomach as it slowed down and stopped. The driver's brown hair...

It looked a heck of a lot like *Benjamin's* hair.

But it couldn't be him.

The Benjamin she knew wouldn't have left the office if a tornado swept through it. He would have chained himself to the desk and kept on working, so there was no way he was *here*, in South Dakota.

Then the door popped open and out he came, wearing an expensive three-piece gray suit, shiny black loafers, and a pair of Gucci shades. He looked as out of place on her farm as he possibly could. Utterly ridiculous. Stupid, even.

And yet the suit hugged his hard biceps and tapered in at his six-pack abs, and *God*, he looked delicious at the same time. And that made her even angrier.

How dare he come here? *How dare he?*

After all he'd done, after how he'd made her feel, he had the nerve to show his face on *her* turf, looking handsome as the devil himself and staring at her as if he'd been as hungry for the sight of her as she'd been for him, which was a big, fat lie.

Just as all the other things he'd told her had been.

She wrapped her arms around herself, not approaching him, and called out, "You can get right back in that car and drive off. You're not welcome here, *Mr. Gale*."

"No." He came around the front of his shiny Cadillac, his jaw hard and his hands curled into fists. God, he looked so good. It wasn't fair. None of this was. "I'm not going anywhere. Not until you hear me out. My messages—"

"You shouldn't have come here." She lifted her chin. "What would Elizabeth say?"

"I don't give a damn what she would say." He had the audacity to look confused. He stopped just short of arm's reach, but close enough for her to smell his familiar cologne. She breathed it in deeply, closing her eyes against the pain it caused and the incredibly strong longing it brought to life. "Why should I?"

"Where is she? Did you tell her you were coming here?"

He blinked. "No. I didn't feel the need to inform her of my whereabouts."

"But you— It doesn't matter." Uncrossing her arms, she backed up. "If you won't go, I will."

"Wait." He caught her arm. She hissed, because his touch burned through the fabric of her shirt, searing her. "Please, Maggie."

"*No*." She yanked free, stumbling back. He made as if to reach for her, but she scowled him off. "Don't touch me."

His fingers flexed, but he remained still. "I bought the farm for your parents. It's safe now. They can stay here, and you can come home to New York."

She shook her head. "I'm not going home, because it's *not* my home. This is. Not that city. New York is for people like you, not me."

"But—" Something that looked a lot like pain crossed his expression. "Did you listen to any of my messages?"

No. And she wouldn't. But she lifted her chin and lied. After all, he was so good at it, so she might as well try her hand at it, too. "Yes. Every one of them. Twice."

His jaw flexed. "And you still hate me, after all that I said?"

She didn't answer him. She couldn't. As hard as she'd tried, she couldn't find it in her heart to hate him because she *loved* him. And that's what made this even worse.

She loved him, and he was engaged to someone else.

"I'm sorry I hurt you." His nostrils flared. "And I meant every word I said in those messages. I'd do anything to go back. To do things differently."

To do what differently?

Never ask me to be your fiancée?

"Just go, Benjamin. It's over."

"I—I see." Reaching out, he brushed his knuckles across her cheekbone, sadness taking over his features. But why would *he* be sad? "I'm sorry, darling. I never meant to hurt you. Or to be like all the other guys in your life. And I never wanted you to hate me."

She closed her eyes, shutting out him and his touch. "Go home, Benjamin. You don't belong here any more than I belong in the city."

"Can't you forgive me? We could at least be friends."

He swallowed. "I don't want to lose you completely, darling. Please."

She shook her head once. "No."

"I'm so fucking sorry, Maggie." His touch lingered, and he moved closer, pressing his mouth against her forehead. "You were my one chance at happiness. My one shot at true love. Guess it just goes to show that guys like me don't deserve love, or happiness. And I certainly don't deserve you."

With that, he got in his car and drove away.

By the time his words pierced through the thick shield of pain surrounding her, he was gone. Wait…had he just said he loved her? That she'd made him happy?

But what about *Elizabeth*? His mother hadn't lied about that. She saw them kissing with her own eyes. So why was he talking about being in love with *Maggie*?

She ran her arm across her forehead, took a deep breath, and pulled her phone out. Swiping her finger across the screen, she opened her voicemail and braced herself to listen to them all. He'd called once a day, every day, and it was time to hear to what he had to say…like she should have done before sending him away.

She hit play on the newest message.

"Hey. It's me again. I hope you're not mad at me for doing what I did. I figured if your parents were safe and settled, maybe you'd be ready to come back home. You don't want to talk to me, and I was an asshole the last time you saw me, but I…" He paused, and she held her breath. "I miss you, Maggie. I miss you so damn much it hurts. I'm alone again, and I should be used to that after being alone for years, but after having you in my life…I'm not. Come home to me. I'll be waiting. I'll wait for you forever, if that's what it takes. You know what? Screw that. I'm coming to you, and I'm not leaving without you unless you tell me to. Even then, I won't give up on you. I need you, darling."

Click.

Hands shaking, she played the second newest message. "I'm miserable without you, Maggie. I'm even more of a beast than before. I'm sorry my mother did what she did to you, and I'm going to fix it. I'm going to save your farm. It's not what you wanted, or what you expected, but I miss you. And I need you to come back to me and be mine again. Please."

Click.

She listened to the rest of the messages, each one more or less the same. He missed her. He wanted her back. He was sorry. He didn't love Elizabeth. He didn't want to marry Elizabeth, and he never had, and she kissed him, not the other way around. It was all a ruse devised by his mother.

Of freaking course.

And she'd fallen for it.

Maggie collapsed into the rocking chair, since her legs would no longer support her, and stared up at the bright blue sky, phone held to her heart. He didn't love Elizabeth. He wasn't with her—and he wanted Maggie to come home to him.

God, she wanted to, because she loved him, and maybe he loved her, too.

Sure, he hadn't said as much, but he'd left her ten messages begging her to come back because he missed her. And he'd taken a break from work, flown out here, and tried to get her to come back when she refused to answer his calls.

If that wasn't love, she wasn't sure what was.

Chapter Eighteen

Benjamin made his way toward the door as he fought through the crowd at the Met, trying his best not to look utterly bored and miserable. But he probably failed because he was both of those things, and he wasn't in the fucking mood to pretend otherwise. While he used to be good at hiding his feelings, lately…well, he sucked ass at it.

He missed Maggie and her smile and her laugh and the way she made *him* laugh. Hell, he missed every damn thing about her. He'd been falling for her before she'd climbed under his table and announced he was her fiancé, and he'd fallen even harder after that. There was no coming back from that, and he didn't want to.

He just wanted *her* to come back—into his arms and never leave again. But she made it pretty damn clear she wouldn't. She was finished with him. Over him.

And he'd never be over her.

Paying off her parents' debt like that had been a gamble. Going to see her had been an even bigger one. She didn't like when he threw his money around, but they had been about to lose their farm, thanks to his mother. He couldn't just do *nothing*. He'd done the right thing.

But she hated him. And he loved her.

Wasn't that just fucking *lovely*?

Pushing the doors open, he stepped out into the cool night air, pulled his phone out of his pocket and checked for a reply from Maggie. A reply he wouldn't get, but that didn't stop him from hoping like a damn fool anyway. He'd sent her another text a couple of hours ago. She'd read it, but hadn't replied.

The story of his life.

Dropping his phone back into his pocket, he sighed and leaned against the railing, staring out into the night. The snow fell from the sky in big flakes, and covered the streets below. Central park was lit up with Christmas lights, and that had always been his favorite part of the elaborate decorations, but he couldn't enjoy it tonight. The city was picturesque at Christmas, but he didn't even care.

He missed Maggie too damn much.

He hadn't been lying when he told her he would wait forever if he had to...but he'd rather it not be that long. They'd already lost enough time together. "I'm coming back to you, and this time, I won't leave until you love me, too," he muttered under his breath. "And now I'm talking to myself, like you. Perfect."

Taking his phone out, he called her. It, of course, went to voicemail. "I shouldn't have left yesterday. I shouldn't have listened to you. You might hate me, and you might never want to see me again, but I'm going to change that. Just watch me."

He laughed and rubbed his jaw.

"I miss you so much that I'm talking to myself now. Yeah. You heard me right. So, guess what? Tomorrow, I'm getting back on a plane, and I'm coming out there. I'm going to find you, kiss you, and never let you go again. And I'm going to make you love me as much as I love you, one way or another, even if it takes a million years. So…there. See you soon. Merry Christmas, darling."

He hung up, smiling for the first time in a week and a half. He was winning his Maggie back. One way or the other… she'd be his. For real, this time.

No make-believe. No pretend rings. Just them.

The door opened, and he stepped to the side to let whoever was exiting enjoy the balcony. When he smiled at them, ready to pass, he froze. "Andrew? What are you doing out here?"

"I wanted to talk to you." Andrew shut the door and leaned against it, his gaze focused on Benjamin. "After what Mother pulled, I feel I owe you an explanation."

Benjamin nodded. "Yeah. Okay."

"I never wanted to take your job, and when Mother had that dinner, I had no idea what I was walking into until it was too late. Next thing I know, she's talking about motions, and people were agreeing with her, and I froze."

Benjamin tried to ignore the dull pain at the idea of his brother silently letting people plot his termination, but it was impossible. "It's okay."

"But I never would have done it. You have to believe me." Andrew stepped forward. "I wouldn't have taken your job. You blame yourself for what happened with Father, but I never did. It happened quickly. It wasn't your fault you weren't there."

"I know. And I believe you."

Andrew blinked. "You do?"

"Yeah."

He sagged against the door again. "Oh, thank God."

"All's well that ends well, right?" Benjamin asked.

"Right."

"Did she tell you her other secret?" he asked.

Andrew cocked his head. "No. What secret?"

"Turns out, I'm not hers." He laughed. "I'm his secretary's son. Dad had an affair, apparently, and got me out of it. Mother covered it up out of shame."

Andrew's jaw dropped. "I had no idea. Are you okay?"

"Yeah. If anything, I'm happy." He shrugged. "It's not as if she loved me. She didn't."

"That's not true," Andrew argued weakly.

He stared at his brother, not arguing. They both knew she hated him. "It doesn't matter, anyway. I'm leaving soon, to find Maggie."

Andrew perked up. "Speaking of which, she's—"

"I'm going to get her back." He stared at Central Park, smiling for the first time in a long time. "No matter how far I have to go, or what I have to do, I will get her back, and she'll forgive me. I won't live my life as miserable as our mother was."

"I bet it won't be as hard as you might think, brother." Andrew opened the door, smiling. "Go get her."

Dragging a hand through his hair, he went back inside, squeezing his brother's shoulder as he passed. The second he stepped foot in the crowded ballroom, women his mother had "personally invited" converged on him, like ants fighting over the last crumb at a picnic. They were wasting their time. He wasn't interested.

Not unless one of them was Maggie.

"I got you a whiskey," a blonde said.

"Can we dance?" a brunette asked. "I love this song."

He tugged on his bowtie and scanned the crowd, looking for the coat check area. "I'm sorry, but I—" He cut off mid-sentence, because he caught a flash of midnight blue. Midnight blue that looked an awful lot like… "*Maggie.*"

It was her. It had to be.

She had her back to him, but he'd recognize her anywhere.

And she was wearing *his* dress. The one he'd bought for her to wear tonight. Her hair was swept up, and tendrils slipped out in artful disarray. She looked hauntingly beautiful.

And he missed her so damn much.

"Maggie," he repeated, unable to believe she was here, in the same room as him. "*Maggie.*"

"No. My name's Julia." A woman reached up and rested her hand on his arm. "Julia Edgerton."

"Let go of me." He shrugged her off, his focus locked on to that flash of blue in the distance. "I have to go."

Ignoring the horrified gasp behind him, he fought his way through the crowd as the clock struck twelve behind him. It was officially Christmas. He elbowed his way toward the vision in blue, his heart pounding so hard it was all he heard. Halfway across the floor, she turned.

He hadn't imagined it. She was there. Standing across the room from him.

"My Maggie," he breathed again, smiling.

As if by magnetism, her gaze latched on to his. Her lips quirked into a tiny smile, and she started across the floor, too. Benjamin sped up his steps, because now that she'd seen him, and he'd seen her, he knew what this meant.

She'd come *home.*

They met in the middle of the floor, and the crowd parted for them, like they sensed something huge was happening here. And it was. If she'd come back to him, he was never letting her go again. He caught her hands in his. "You're here. You came home to me."

She turned her face up to him, all bright smiles and shining gray eyes with blue specks. "Did you ever think I wouldn't?"

"Well…yeah." He let out a laugh. "After you sent me home alone, I kind of did."

She laughed, too. "Fair enough. I shouldn't have sent you

away. I lied. I hadn't listened to those messages."

"Oh." He paused, running his thumb over the back of her knuckles. It felt as if it had been years since he'd been able to touch her, and he'd been starving for it. Having her in his arms made the earth stop trembling, and it was as if he'd never let her go in the first place. All the fear, pain, and hurt faded away. "Are you still mad at me?"

She shook her head once. "Nope."

"Good." He stepped closer. "Can you forgive me for being an asshole that day? I'd just found out I lost everything—which was a lie, but I'll get to that later. And you were leaving, and I thought it was because—"

She pressed two fingers against his lips. "I have no idea what you're talking about, but yes. I forgive you. Do you forgive me for believing your mother's lies in the first place, and for not telling you the whole story when you came to see me?"

"Maggie…" He hauled her into his arms and hugged her so tight she squealed. "What do you think?"

"I think you should kiss me," she whispered.

Relief and desire surged through him, warring with one another for control. "Darling? I thought you'd never ask."

The second his lips touched hers, the past week and a half faded away. She'd never left, and he'd never lost her, and they were *happy*. He fisted the soft fabric of her dress, inhaled deeply, and forced himself to step back when all he wanted was to pull her closer. But not here, where they couldn't finish what they started. Once he started…

She wouldn't be getting out of his bed for hours. Days, even.

"I missed you so damn much," he whispered into her ear, swaying to the music since they were in the middle of the dance floor. "Everything about you haunted me, killed me, hurt me. This all started with a lie, and was for pretend, but please don't *ever* leave me like that again."

She tightened her grip on his tux jacket and nodded. "I missed you, too. So much."

"I lo—" He broke off, shaking his head. "Shit. Not here. There's so much to say. Will you come home with me?"

Nodding, she smiled. "Yes. I'll go home with you, Benji."

"Good. But first..." He cleared his throat. "Maggie Donovan, will you do me the honor of being my girlfriend?"

She let out a little laugh. "No more fake fiancée or diamond rings?"

"No. Mother and I had a little talk, and I went above her head about the stunt she pulled." He tucked a loose strand of hair behind her ear ad kissed her temple. "Needless to say, my position is currently very secure, and she got a slap on the wrist."

"Should have gotten more. Or at the very least, I should've been the one to do it," she muttered under her breath. Then, out loud, she said, "Uh...I mean, *good*."

"And next time I give you a ring, it'll be for real." He pulled back and locked eyes with her, still dancing. "I want to spend the rest of my life with you. Loving you. Holding you."

Her breath caught in her throat, and she smiled at him.

He splayed his hand across the small of her back. "Be mine, darling. For real this time. No more games. No lies. Just us. Together."

"Just us," she echoed, cupping his cheek. "Yes, Benji."

He smiled so big he probably looked ridiculous, but he didn't give a damn. He didn't even care that she'd used that annoying nickname again. It was music to his ears. The clock finished chiming, and he pulled her even closer. It still wasn't close enough. "I've never been so happy to hear that ridiculous name as I am now."

"By the way?" Leaning up on tiptoe, she whispered in his ear, "I'm naked under this dress. Completely. Naked."

His cock came to life, painfully and insistently, reminding him just how much he'd missed her, in every possible way. Screw *dancing*. It was time to go home. "*Maggie*."

When she just grinned and held her hand out for him, he grabbed it and dragged her toward the door. They made it outside and into the limo in record time. He didn't even care that he left his coat behind. Screw it. He had plenty.

There was only one Maggie Donovan, though.

The second the door closed behind them, he pulled her onto his lap, pounded on the glass of the limo he'd rented for the night, and called out, "Home, Jeff."

His driver pulled away from the curve, and Benjamin brought his mouth to hers, kissing her as if she alone could save him. And he had a feeling that was true.

He'd learned as much when she'd walked away from him.

She slid her tongue into his mouth, moaning while he shoved her dress out of his way, baring the pale skin he'd dreamt about every night for the past three weeks. He skimmed his fingers over her soft thighs, slipping them inward as he arched his hips up.

"I thought I'd never get to touch you like this again." He tightened his hold on her, kissing the side of her temple. "I'm so sorry I hurt you. So damn sorry."

"It's okay." She cradled his face and smiled down at him. "We just had our first fight, that's all."

He closed the distance between them, his mouth brushing against hers ever so slightly. "And we made it through."

"Yep." She entwined her hands with his. "Together."

He grinned. "Together."

"I'm not saying it's going to be easy. I mean, we're still very different. And your mother is still going to hate me, and she'll still try to get you kicked out for picking me. And she'll still make our life a living hell because—"

"I don't give a damn. Not anymore." He laughed because

it was true, and the knowledge that she no longer held any sort of power over him was so fucking freeing. Maggie had helped him get that freedom, and he'd never be able to thank her enough for that. "Besides, she's not even really my mother."

Maggie's jaw dropped. "Wait. What?"

"I'll tell you the story." He tucked her hair behind her ear. "But I don't want to talk about that now. All that matters is here and now. Us."

Her wide eyes pinned him, searching his soul. "But are you okay?"

"I'm fucking ecstatic because you're *here*." He smiled. "I'm not familiar with the emotion, but if you let me, I'll love you with all of my heart, mind, body, soul, and life. And even after that, I'll keep on loving you, darling. I swear it. I love you so damn much, Maggie. So. Damn. Much."

Her eyes widened. "You…you're…I…"

"It's okay. I know it's quick and all." He laughed and kissed her. "You don't have to say anything back. I'll wait. I'm a patient man."

"But—" She shook her head and slowly, beautifully, a smile spread across her face. "I love you, too."

He froze. "You do?"

"I do."

"Well, shit." He laughed and kissed her, keeping it short. "That officially makes me the happiest guy on earth. Where's my trophy?" He cupped the back of her neck. "Oh. Right. She's here, in my arms already." He lowered her face to his, stopping just short of kissing her. "Say it again, darling."

She fisted his tux, her breath hitching in her throat. "I love you, Benji."

"I love you, too."

Unable to resist, the happiness practically bursting out of him, he pulled her down for a passionate, long, deep kiss. And he never wanted to stop. But then the limo *did*.

He picked her up and set her down, straightening her dress over her thighs. "You good, darling?"

"Y-Yeah." Maggie watched him, smoothing her hair. "We're home, aren't we?"

Home. Such a simple word that held so much meaning. He'd found his home, but it wasn't in the traditional sense. He'd found it in *her*. He opened the door and climbed out, offering her his hand. "Yeah. We're home."

She slid her fingers into his, grinning as she followed him out. They walked into the building hand-in-hand, and come what may—whatever they might have to face or fight their way through—they could make it.

Together.

Epilogue

Laughter rang out all around the living room's pale yellow walls, and someone called out *bullshit* from the dining room, where a rousing game of cards was being waged. If Benjamin had learned anything during his weeklong stay here at Maggie's farm, it was that her family took competition *very* seriously.

Even if it was "friendly."

After the first time he'd beaten her father at cards—and had consequently feared for his life—he decided to avoid those games until he was liked enough not to be shot on the spot for winning. He was already almost there. Her family had greeted him with open arms and warm smiles. It was so foreign. So different. So *welcome*.

Staring into the crackling fireplace, he shifted his weight on the couch. He'd never been so accepted, so *happy*, as he'd been this last week, in South Dakota of all places. His "mother" was still a thorn in their sides they did their best to ignore, but being away from her—and all the drama she brought with her—had been paradise.

He almost didn't want to go back. Life could be good here.

They could take over the farm from her parents and raise a bunch of gorgeous little brown-haired Maggies amidst the crops and the open, never-ending plains. He could be happy here. And so could Maggie.

Someone sat down beside him, and he didn't need to look to find out who. He'd recognize her scent anywhere. Maggie wrapped her arms around him, resting her cheek on his shoulder. "Whatcha thinking about?"

He held on to her wrists with one hand. The other held on to his beer. His heart picked up speed, because he was actually thinking about this. About walking away from their life in New York, and his company, and becoming a fucking farmer. "Have you ever thought about moving back out here?"

"Yeah, sometimes. I mean, it's my home. Of course I think about it." She stiffened. "Why? What's wrong?"

"Nothing," he said quickly. He chugged the rest of his beer and pulled her onto his lap. She squealed and threw her arms around his neck. "Nothing's wrong, and that's just what I was thinking about."

She grinned and smoothed his messy hair. "Don't worry, I'm not going anywhere. You're stuck with me."

"I don't think I'd use the word 'stuck.' *Blessed*, maybe." He nuzzled her neck and breathed in her scent, letting it soothe his nerves. "You make me so happy, Maggie. Happier than I'd have ever thought possible, or even believed in. I love you."

"I love you, too," she whispered.

Her gaze dipped down, lighting up with appreciation. She

wriggled in his lap, brushing her sweet ass against his hard cock. Around her, he was always hard. Like a fast food joint, he was open twenty-four hours a day and ready to serve her at a moment's notice. "Watch yourself," he warned, nipping at her throat.

"I can't help it." She trailed her fingers down the buttons of his shirt. "You might not be *the* beast anymore, but you're one *hot* beast in a flannel, jeans, and a five o'clock shadow. Who knew South Dakota would suit you so well?"

He rolled his hips up, his attention on the door to the living room. Maggie's parents were the opposite of his mother—loving and kind and embracing—so they wouldn't be alone much longer. "I can show you just how well it suits me, right now, in our room."

She watched him through her dark lashes. "Oh...?"

"Yeah." He stood up, holding her in his arms. "I have something to show you outside first, though."

She blinked at him. "But it's snowing and freezing."

"Don't worry. I'll keep you warm." He set her on her feet and wrapped a blanket around her shoulders. His legs felt a little bit weaker than normal, but he ignored that. "Come with me?"

"Okaaaay." She eyed him as if he'd gone a little mad, and maybe he had. "Let's go, then."

He'd spoken with her father earlier today, and it was almost midnight, which meant it was almost Christmas, which made this their official one-year anniversary—and he knew exactly how he wanted to celebrate it. And where.

He threw his arm over her shoulder and led her to the front door, winking at her father as they left. Glen nodded once, and whispered something to her mother—who covered her mouth. Maggie missed all of this.

She was too busy watching him with a wrinkled brow.

"Are you feeling okay?" She stopped on the porch and

rested a hand on his forehead. "You look a little green."

"I'm fine." He pulled her hand down and held on to it for dear life. "Come on. I want to show you something."

She followed him, shivering, but didn't argue. When they reached the huge willow tree in the middle of the backyard, he stopped, smiling up at the dark sky. Snowflakes fell, drifting down slowly and magically. "It's snowing."

"Yeah." She glanced up at the sky for two seconds, but her gaze came back to him. "What's going on? Why are you acting so strange?"

"Give me a second. I need to work it all out in my head. It has to be perfect." He let out a soft chuckle and brushed her hair out of her eyes. "You deserve perfect, darling."

She nibbled on her lower lip. "Okaaaaaayyyyy."

Turning to face her, he rubbed her slim arms through the blanket. He could feel her goose bumps even through the thick material. "This past year has been heaven, Maggie. Pure heaven. You gave me myself—and helped me remember the kind of man I wanted to be. A man who loved, and laughed, and *lived*. I love you so damn much. You have no idea."

She smiled. "I love you, too, Benji."

"But you don't understand. I didn't really live until *you*. I existed as a shadow of myself, sure, but that's not the same." He caught both of her hands and held on tight, smiling. "You taught me that, just like you taught me what real love feels like."

Awareness dawned on her, as if she figured out why they were out here, in the cold. He saw it in her expression. "Benjamin..."

"You are my everything. My life. My love. My heart." He squeezed her hands and laughed, because tears rolled down her cheeks. "Do you know what this tree is?"

She nodded, not speaking.

"Then you know that your father brought your mother out

here, when they first started dating, and they planted the tree together. He told her that the tree would grow, like his love for her, and that he wanted to spend the rest of his life with her." He let go of her hands, wiped the tears off her cheeks, and reached into his pocket. "This is where he asked her to marry him. The tree was a lot smaller, but you get the idea."

She covered her mouth. "Oh my God."

"Maggie Louise Donovan, you have made me the happiest man on this earth, so I might be getting greedy now, asking for more, but I'm going to do it anyway." He sank to one knee and pulled out a little blue box—one she probably recognized all too well. "You are the one person I never have to wonder about, the one person I always want by my side. Will you make me an even happier man and agree to be my wife? To spend the rest of our lives together—here or in New York, I don't give a damn, as long as I have you—loving one another? No matter what comes?"

She fell to her knees in front of him and kissed him. She tasted like tears and sunshine—and forever. By the time she pulled back, his vision was less than perfectly clear. He blinked rapidly, grinning as she sniffed loudly and said, "I love you. I love you so much."

He nodded. "But you still have to answer me."

"Oh my—" She laughed and covered her mouth. "Well, I can only think of one appropriate reply." She rested her hands on his shoulders, giving him the brightest smile he'd ever seen. "I thought you'd never ask, Benji."

She threw herself at him, and they fell to the ground, lips locked. The ring tumbled somewhere in the snow, but neither of them broke off long enough to search for it. She eventually ended the kiss, resting her forehead on his. "I can't believe you knew about this tree. How did you find out about it?"

"Like a wise person once told me…" He tucked her hair behind her ear and craned his neck, searching for the blue box. He found it easily. "Research. Always research."

She cupped his face. "I love you, Benji."

"I love you, too. And I meant what I said." He pulled the ring out with a trembling hand. "I'll move out here with you, if that's what you want. We can be farmers and live here and keep the family business going. This farm means a lot to your family—and to me, too."

"What about *your* family business?"

"That doesn't seem as important as it did a year ago. Probably because my mother isn't really my family. You are." He kissed her again and held out the ring. "I love you."

She blinked away tears and took it. "I love you, too."

"Read it."

"What?" She picked it up and held it to the moonlight, squinting. "Forever yours, for all time, Benji."

He took it from her and slid it on, watching the way it fit as he did so. It was the same ring as before—he'd planned to give it back to her someday, for real this time, so it wasn't the first time he'd seen it on her. But it was the first time it meant something. Something real. And he'd never been happier. "Seeing that on you...it does things to me, darling. I was alone for so long."

"You're not alone. Not anymore." She wrapped her arms around him and straddled him, face to face. "And never again."

"Because of you." He rubbed noses with her. Hers was freezing. "Because of *us*."

She kissed him again, and he pulled her closer against his chest, wrapping the blanket around the both of them. It still wasn't close enough. Nothing ever would be. Not for this beast and the beauty who had saved him from himself. By the time they came up for air, the kiss had taken on a whole new meaning.

It was a beginning. A promise. A vow.

Of *forever*.

Acknowledgments

I've written lots of books, and with that, lots of acknowledgements. But this time, I want to keep it short and sweet, and say thank you to those of you out there who have read those books. Whether this is your twentieth book by me, or your first…

THANK YOU.

Without you, I wouldn't be able to do this.

About the Author

Diane Alberts is a multi-published, bestselling contemporary romance author with Entangled Publishing. She also writes *New York Times*, *USA Today*, and *Wall Street Journal* bestselling new adult books under the name Jen McLaughlin. She's hit the Top 100 lists on Amazon and Barnes and Noble numerous times with numerous titles. She was mentioned in *Forbes* alongside E. L. James as one of the breakout independent authors to dominate the bestselling lists. Diane is represented by Louise Fury at The Bent Agency.

Don't miss the Modern Fairytales series...

THE PRINCE'S BRIDE

Discover more romance from Entangled...

OVER HER WED BODY
a novel by Alexia Adams

Beckett Samuelson can spot a gold digger when he sees one. So when his ailing father announces his engagement to the private nurse he's only known for two months, Beckett has to step in. Before long he realizes he realizes she's the perfect next Mrs. Samuelson. If only he was the intended groom...

HOW NOT TO MESS WITH A MILLIONAIRE
a Mediterranean Millionaires novel by Regina Kyle

Interior decorator Zoe Ryan's life resembles a country song. What's a girl to do? Leave everything behind for a bit...in Italy. When she gets there, she finds a surprise—millionaire restaurateur Dante Sabbatini in the kitchen. In his underwear. Making coffee. It's suddenly not only hot outside... but what is he doing inside, in her temporary kitchen? The very thing, it seems, that she's trying to avoid, and resisting is impossible.

NO PLAYER REQUIRED
a Biggest Little Love Story novel by JoAnn Sky

Billionaire casino magnate Rafael "Rafa" Salord is forced to exchange caviar for cowboy boots when he's sent to "grow up" and run his father's newly acquired casino in the middle of nowhere downtown Reno. When he crosses paths with feisty Destiny Morson, he starts to wonder if that nonsense about love-at-first-sight might actually be true. Maybe it's time to trade in his playboy status and bet on something more.